Kangana

Punam Farmah

Kangana

Cover art 'Colours on the wind'
Punam Farmah Copyright © 2018
ISBN-10: 172512131X
ISBN-13: 978-1725121317

Also by Punam Farmah:

Playing with Plant Pots: Tales from the allotment

Sow, Grow and Eat: From plot to kitchen

Fragments

**Retreating to Peace: A Peace Series
Novella**

Kangana

Kangana

Kangana

For my heaven-sent wing-people:

Surrinder, Howard, Michelle and Sharlene

Kangana

ACKNOWLEDGMENTS

This book wouldn't have happened without Surrinder Sihota and all of her advice and guidance.

Without all of the lovely ladies in the Peace Novella Series, I wouldn't have had the courage to write this.

Doctors Ravjeet Kour and Salmah Yakob who provided the encouragement and cheer-leading to stop me from going mad when plotting an idea.

Amo, you really are one of my favourite people. Without you there would be no sunshine and vibrancy in this book.

Last but not least. He of all the pies; Doctor Sotiris Skandalis. 'Hallelujah' is the soundtrack to some of the bits and pieces that happen. After all these years, you are officially in a book.

Kangana

Punam Farmah

Prologue

"Your feet are freezing," Gorbind winced as his own feet recoiled from Padmi's toes. Toes that also need clipping; there were raw, very angry-feeling grazes across his shins. She had dragged her big toe from just behind his knee all the way towards his ankle in sadistic, sockless, seduction.

"The rest of me is pretty warm though," Padmi uttered softly. "You might want to make the most of it; five year anniversary and all."

Gorbind didn't need to be told twice as he shifted sideways into the middle of double bed with his arm outstretched. It took Padmi all of three seconds to do the same. As she rolled into his arms, Gorbind held his breath. Her head was sat against chest as she wrapped his arms around her. Her curves and contours were locked into place alongside his. He saw her close her eyes, before snaking her leg diagonally across his knees to clamp him closer still.

"Five years," Muttered Gorbind, he had his eyes firmly closed. His nose nudged into Padmi's crown of dark, damp hair to inhale the scent of coconut and lime. A scent, that rather made him smile. "Five years ago, it would have been unthinkable that you might invade my shower with me in it. It never occurred to me, that you might pinch my shampoo, pass judgement on my choice of shower gel. I don't even like coconut and lime, but it does make you smell good enough to eat. Five years on, and it all it took was a badly made cup of tea."

"Wasn't my fault," Padmi tutted. There was further movement below decks as she poked his left thigh with her toe. "I blame the machine. Who in their right mind drinks vending machine tea?"

"I was hungover," Gorbind would make no apologies for grumbling. "Nine a.m. lecture on a Monday morning, I'd rolled out of bed too late to make a proper, fresh batch. All that drinking over RAG week completely totalled my faculties."

"Not just *your* faculties," Padmi yawned, sweeping a veil of hair from across her face. "Everyone else's faculties took something of a hit too."

Gorbind started to laugh quietly, his shoulders

bobbing up and own. "You turned up, in the biggest, ugliest pair of shades ever. Mid-October, yet you looked like a dramatic Greta Garbo. You were flouncing everywhere. The piece de resistance you thumped the machine as it wouldn't respond to your aggravated poking," he curled a finger, jabbed it playfully into where Padmi's back curved into a well-proportioned, beautifully curved backside.

"You never did give me that ninety pence," Padmi smirked; she was tracing her toe across her knee, making the hairs on the back of his neck stand up. "Just drank your tea whilst trying not to make eye contact; you didn't half go a bit pink. Eventually, you told me that you could make better tea with your eyes closed. Then you asked if I wanted one."

"For some daft reason, you nearly smacked me one!" scoffed Gorbind, his shoulders rising in protest. "How dare you!" he continued, mimicking Padmi's elongated, private school vowels. "Nine in the morning, you could've bought me dinner before being so vulgar and forward."

"God, you looked mortified," Padmi giggled, her toes were once more moving towards his shin. "You went proper beetroot, stormed off without so much as a see you later."

"I did catch up with you eventually." Gorbind nodded slowly. "That was by far, the most bizarre episode ever," he said unable to stop grinning. "The two of us talking at cross-purposes. What was it, that I eventually said? How about a cup of tea, a proper one? I'll think about dinner." He reeled off what had felt a perfectly innocuous, boring sentence.

"Yep, I asked you to define proper," replied Padmi, sitting up a little to tower over him slightly; she looked down into his eyes. Edging closer, he felt the end of his nose collide with hers.

"Hot, spicy, and full of oomph," his worlds tumbled out quickly. Padmi gave him no time to breathe as she claimed his lips for her own. She then proceeded to uncurl her curves from his contours, dragging him over to what she called her side of the bed.

"Remind me, would you," Padmi's arms were hooked around his neck; her legs snaked around his waist. "The hot, spicy, full of oomph, was that you?" she asked chuckling quietly. "Or was that the tea? It's been five years; a girl can easily forget that sort of thing."

Rolling his eyes, Gorbind feigned despair with a palm at his brow. He remembered the bad chat up line; he remembered the badly made, vending machine tea. Neither was important right now; what mattered, was reminding Padmi of how this whole adventure had started.

Engulfed in her embrace, the scent of coconut and lime gave way to hot, spicy, and full of oomph.

Reminiscing took effort. There was an intensity that pulled Gorbind into the depths of pure, unadulterated intoxication. Spent and soul-devoured, he dozed in and out of sleep as midnight struck. Gorbind lay bewitched in Padmi's arms. There was far too much adrenaline rushing around his system, making it harder for him to surrender unto silent slumbering.

"What you thinking about?" Gorbind's train of thought was derailed by Padmi's words. Then there were the circles that she was drawing with her fingers on his sweaty, salty collar bone.

"I'm thinking about you, me," he said softly, "Standing in the kitchen of halls. I can't forget the smell of Chai Masala. I kept looking at you, whilst wanting to dive into your arms, right there, right then. I had no idea how to talk to you about anything but spices. All I could do was watch you glide across a kitchen that was barely big enough to swing a cat."

"So that's why you looked so goggle-eyed!" Padmi laughed wickedly; pressing her lips together she gently kissed his breastbone and slowly made her way up towards his neck.

He felt his heart thud against hers. The rhythm of the beats was somewhat comforting; two hearts were beating in almost perfect synchronicity. Gorbind's soul tingled; it tingled now as much, if not more than it had at the vending machine.

"Wasn't all bad," said Padmi. She paused her kisses as she arrived at his nose. "I've not had a good first date since. You must have done something right, my sweet." Her hands travelled to his, pinning him to the mattress for another round of rapture.

There had been more dates, lots of them. In five years, so much happened between them; the whole thing was something of a rich, vibrant, passion-filled tapestry of events. He and Padmi had experienced moments of sheer bliss; there had been moments of madness too. He had loved each and every episode; Gorbind had loved Padmi. Padmi has robbed him of his heart, his soul, of everything in between. She had landed in his bed, and all because of some badly made tea. As for the ninety pence, he would be in her debt to his dying day. She was worth far more than a few pieces of silver. Padmi was worth his whole world.

CHAPTER 1

In something of a panicked hurry, Gorbind clambered up the white and grey steps. Flanked by dark-wood balustrades, the steps snaked up to the first floor of the museum and art gallery. He wasn't *just* late, he was *very* late. He should have been here forty minutes ago. Only his car had died a sudden death and refused to move from its parking space in the street. Gorbind had kicked his car-the front tyre anyway-stubbed his toe, and now struggled to move quickly.

Having tried to assault his car, he had ran for bus and annoy the toe further. Fortunately for him, the bus into town had been on time. Not knowing how much he cash he had, turning out his pockets whilst holding up two ladies en-route to bingo had not been pleasant.

As he arrived on the first floor, his trainers squeaked across orange and red floor tiles. Looking up, Gorbind caught sight of Epstein's sculpture of Lucifer. The Fallen Angel stood firmly in the middle of The Round Room. Standing in front of the statue was Padmi; she looked none too pleased as she jabbed furiously as her 'phone.

Gorbind' own 'phone started to ring. An electrified version of 'she's the one' burst through the air. Fumbling into his pocket, he swore quietly under his breath.

Padmi heard the song. She span around to face him with her 'phone pressed to her ear. Her face was thunderous, suggesting that she was about to unleash the dogs of war that would drag Gorbind to hell.

"I can explain," he said bundling his 'phone away to make a grab for her wrist. "That check engine light that you noticed," Gorbind desperately tried to catch his breath as his words tumbled out. "It came on again. The car died, Padmi. The car died a bloody death. Ooh, look, Lucifer!" he exclaimed, looking past her shoulder. "He's a cretin. Me, not so much. I'm positively, properly, angelic in comparison."

Padmi pulled away, Gorbind uncurled his fingers from her arm. He gulped to take a step back. Lucifer towered over them both. As she moved, Padmi stood below the protective reach of the fallen angel's wings.

Slinking his hands into his pockets, Gorbind hunched up his shoulders to brace himself.

"I'm sorry," he offered softly, squinting his eyes to give some impression of remorse. He could see Padmi's brow crease. Her lips pursed tightly together in a rather indignant pout. Sadly, Gorbind knew that face.

That was Padmi's "I'm cheesed off, ready to lamp you, but I'm listening, so talk quick' face. Her glare had a drill-like quality and it was boring straight through him. The way in which Padmi looked at him rather made his heart buzz a little. If his heart were to beat any faster, there was a small danger it might burst through his chest to fall with a splat at her feet.

He wouldn't mind if it did. There was no one else on this planet that he would rather surrender his heart to, or his soul for that matter.

All she had to do was ask.

His hearts was hers.

Gorbind's heart beat only for her.

"Yes?" Padmi turned her head slightly, cupped her ear in anticipation.

Her movement had rather buffeted his train of thought. There was an intrigued burr to her question that nudged him back into reality.

"Epstein modelled Lucifer's head on that of a woman," replied Gorbind. "The rest of him, her, is male," he said, as he shuffled across the tiled floor. He threaded his arm around Padmi's so that they both stood under the broad span of Lucifer's bronze wings.

"Had to cover his bits too," Gorbind waggled a finger at the figure's loin cloth that only just protected the angel's would be modesty. "Lest all the ladies were offended; such was the Victorian morality of the time. Epstein was always going to offend someone at some point."

"Since when were you a tour guide?" asked Padmi, sliding her hands towards his. Gorbind's fingers had returned to his pockets; she liberated his fingers from the frayed lining of his jeans. "You're something of a closet History and Art geek. You kept that quiet, didn't you," she laughed quietly, pulling his hand from his pocket. Her fingers were warm as she wove them between hers. There was something comforting about her touch; comforting about the way it felt as though she didn't want to let go.

"Since I'd spend the first Saturday of every month standing right here with Nani," replied Gorbind. "Arjun would be here too. I came here from about the age of six to about twelve." He inhaled deeply, letting the air inflate his chest to get some buoyancy. "I don't tell many people this. After Mum died, Dad was useless; even more useless than he is now." He spat out the words, his face contorting into a grimace. The mere mention of his father made bile rise in his throat.

"So each month, Nani would bring us both here on the bus, just to get us out of the house; to give us a change of scenery, I guess. We'd stand here, with Lucifer," Gorbind waggled a finger at the sculpture. "She'd make us go through all of the galleries, look at everything," he turned slightly to face Padmi, his eye's widening in emphasis. "We'd get home and she'd make us write about it-practice your English, she'd say-so yes, I am a geek. Don't knock it. Any queries, take them up with Nani."

"This place is really very special," he said turning back to face Lucifer. "One of the few places in this world that make me feel safe, feel happy and human."

"Other than the Gurdwara?" asked Padmi.

"Saving that," grinned Gorbind, another quiet laugh escaped his lips. He could do that with Padmi. As long as she didn't make him cry, she could do with him anything she wanted; Gorbind wouldn't complain. "And for the next date, should we survive this one. But yes," he nodded briefly. "I'd forgotten I'd told you about that. C'mere a minute. You have to see the rest of the round room." Still holding her hand firmly in hers, Gorbind tugged her towards the curved wall behind them.

"I'm not going to Gurdwara for a third date, Gorbind," protested Padmi. Loudly at that too, her words bounced off the floor to thud against his chest. The gallery was almost empty with no bodies to act as buffers to her complaint.

As Gorbind pulled Padmi past a maroon banquette his shoes continued to squeak across the floor. He looked down momentarily; the red, blue, purple and grey mosaic was actually still quite pretty given its vintage.

Just not as pretty as the woman from whose arm he was currently dangling.

He had led Padmi to the wall labelled 'Imagining the past' before letting go of her hand. He placed two hands to her shoulders to shuffle her directly in front of a panorama of Ancient Greeks. A third of the image was made up of an ivory coloured colonnade. In the foreground, dressed in ochre, orange and green tunics and robes was an Athenian audience. Laurel leaves littered the white marble floor before them. The figures looked as though they were waiting with baited breath; as though they were waiting for the couple to explain themselves.

"Athenians," Gorbind whispered into her ear. "All wanting to know, whether you have been up to no good." Sliding his hands slowly down her arms, passed her elbows, his fingers landed into hers. "They want every detail, every last bit of naughtiness you are guilty of: every line crossed. They'd quite like to hear it all. Tell them, tell me. What you say, won't go any further. How about it?"

He could see the tip of her teeth bite into her lip. Would she, would she share? There was still so much they still had to learn about each other. He was so close, he could smell the top notes of the perfume that clung to her skin.

"Drama Queen!" exclaimed Padmi, breaking the moment. Her elbow jolted back to poke into his stomach.

"Oof, hey, no fair," he groaned, rubbing a palm in a circular motion where her elbow had impacted. "Tell me, else I will throw you to the lions," he raised an index finger to waggle it above at the image of a man tangling with a lion. "Phoebus Apollo, one angry looking fella," said Gorbind. "…and an even angrier gang of lions."

Padmi rolled her eyes towards the lions before returning to the Athenians. "They don't half look miserable," she said wrinkling up her nose. "If this whole place is full of miserable, Ancient Greeks, Gorbind, you and I will fall out and then some. I can't guarantee that I won't throw *you* to the lions, never mind a bunch of dead guys."

"They're dead," Gorbind shrugged. "Won't matter one bit to them. I, on the other hand, would quite like to stay alive. Moving swiftly on," he took her once more by the hand to shuffle-squeak across the tiles. This time, he stood Padmi by a greyer, more sombre image.

"That one," he flicked an index finger towards two women sat on a stone wall with a steely blue seascape behind them. The younger of two women, a red-head, held her head in her hands whilst the other put a palm gently on her shoulder. "Listen, lovey," Gorbind pinched his tone to affect the pitch and burr of an age-wearied crone, complete with a crackle and sour sharpness. "Any boy who wears socks with sandals really does need a personality transplant. Then there is the woolly jumpers..." As he had spoken, his tone had risen; he found it too difficult to keep a straight face whilst staying in character. "Looks like he wearing an acid trip. Looking at him for just two minutes don't half make your eyes go funny."

"How about you?" Padmi turned around in his arms to face him. "Are you worth it, are you going to make me cry?"

"Yes," he replied shuffling forward, his feet moved either side of hers. He looked down to make sure didn't step on Padmi's toes. "And no," he added looking directly into her eyes. "No plans to ever knowingly or unknowingly make you cry. I don't want to hurt you, but…."

"But?" Padmi's eyes narrowed, the colour appeared to drain from her face.

Gorbind felt his stomach lurch.

"If you ever make me watch that God-awful telenovella again," laughed Gorbind, stepping back to avoid the hand raised to swat him one across his shoulder.

Padmi managed to land a blow across his bicep before he scuttled away. "I like to see the costumes!" she tutted as she shook her head. "No one wears those saris, all that bling on a daily basis in real life."

"Saris?! Don't make me laugh," Gorbind made a grab to reclaim her hands. "You just like to perv over the brooding boys with slicked back hair. Then there are the dodgy camera angles and funny sound effects. C'mon, there's more. Pretty Raphaelites," he said leading her on further. "Now those girls really are pretty."

"Pretty, what do you mean, pretty?!" Padmi's words bounced against the walls once more. Ignoring her, Gorbind led her further into the bowels of the gallery.

Gorbind's shoes squeaked against pale blonde parquet

flooring as they entered the bridge gallery. Beyond this were the Pre-Raphaelites; a section of the gallery that he could probably find in his sleep. So much so, there was child-like glee, a spring in his step that couldn't be contained. He might as well have been a six-year old let loose on an adventure. With teal walls, the Pre-Raphaelites were a whole different universe compared to The Round Room.

"The Pre-Raphaelites movement was a strike against boredom," declared Gorbind as they arrived. He shuffled them both into a very specific corner. "Victorian paintings were considered by some to be dour, rigid and downright moralistic. Bit like Alice in wonderland really."

"Alice in wonderland?" Asked Padmi, wearing something of a quizzical look. "The kids book?"

Gorbind hung her left, almost sitting on her shoulder. They both stood before a portrait of a red-haired woman dressed in green, holding what looked like a pomegranate.

"Yep, that's the one," nodded Gorbind. "Padmi, meet Prosperine by Dante Gabriel Rosetti," he pointed to the image behind her. "The first red-head that I had ever clapped eyes on. When you're six years old, have never seen such brightly coloured hair it does rather make you pay attention. She's beautiful," he sounded as though he was about fall over swooning.

18

Tilting her head to the left, Padmi turned on her heel to take a look. She studied the painting closely through narrowed eyes. "Reminds me of that woman, the singer. What was her name, Florence?" she asked, looking over her shoulder; her lashes fluttered to focus much like the lens of a camera.

Gorbind smiled, he could almost hear the clicks of a figurative shutter. "The one with the machine? Now you mention it, I guess she does," he couldn't help but nod. "If you squint hard enough. God only knows what she's thinking. This Prosperine, is the Perserphone of Greek Mythology. Gets dragged to the underworld and stays there for six months of the year. Or so the legend goes.

He felt his arm being gently tugged.

"Come back, Gorbind," Padmi whispered, pulling him closer. "You've gone all misty-eyed, Time Lord again. Am I supposed to hunt down a T.A.R.D.I.S for Christmas? Not sure that would fit into a stocking."

"Stocking?" That brought him back into the room. A rather lupine grin was blooming across his face. He cheeks reddened, forming something of a flush beneath grainy stubble that he forgot to get rid of in his panic to get here. "Never mind buying me a T.A.R.D.I.S. I know what looks better in a stocking. Needn't be Christmas either; that was one hell of a birthday."

They both knew what he was talking about. They had drifted close enough to start dancing if they so wished. All they needed now was the sound of a rumba.

"Maybe," he said quietly, his lips hovering inches from her ear. "I could have two birthdays, like The Queen."

"I bet Persephone had some posh stockings," Padmi grinned, as his nose touched hers. "Not some run of the mill things. There would have to be some seriously posh stockings, if you were to have two birthdays."

Quick time, that was the only way to describe the beating of his heart; it was racing. Ordinarily, it beat quick enough to keep him standing up right. The rhythm could be described as being boorish at best. Now, with Padmi in his arms; her body heat causing her scent to stir his soul, a crescendo rose behind his breast bone.

"I can do posh," Gorbind spoke in the faintest of whispers. He noticed that a lock of thick, black hair had escaped from behind Padmi's ear. He did the gentlemanly thing to tuck it back. The next thing he knew, Padmi had slid her hands from his hips to his shoulder blades. "With bells on, if necessary."

"That really would wake the neighbours," Her one

hand moved to his collar bone, her finger ran gently across the curve of his shoulder. "Never mind the bells, Gorbind. What I want, Gorbind, is you. The stockings would be bonus."

Reaching its peak, the crescendo carried Gorbind forward; his lips met with hers. Words were of no use at this moment in time. He didn't care that they were in the middle of a museum; he didn't mind that a passing parent hurriedly dragged away a rather curious child.

Gorbind made a mental note to go shopping. Stockings wouldn't buy themselves. He could muster up that much, plus anything else that Padmi might need for his two birthdays.

CHAPTER 2

"We're late," Gorbind looked at his watch as Arjun stepped out of the car. "If only you'd got ready a little quicker, we wouldn't have this problem, now would we." There was an agitated edge to Gorbind's tone as he squeezed the fob on his car keys to secure the vehicle. "One blue shirt, pretty much looks like the rest of your shirts, Arjun."

Arjun glared back at him, shaking his head as they walked towards the entrance of The Bulls Head. As the sun was out, smokers lined the decked area outside to take advantage. Most of the tables and chairs were taken, the pub looked rather busy.

"You'd be equally pissed if I didn't make an effort," Arjun countered. "This is the first time I've been asked to meet your girlfriend. All the others were elbowed away before I was ever needed. Excuse me, for wanting to make a good impression."

Gorbind rolled his eyes whilst pushing open the pub door. The bar was on his left, thronging with people elbowing each other. On his right, there was a rather sparsely occupied dining area. He scanned the tables and chairs; a knot was starting to form as Gorbind desperately searched for Padmi. It took a while; Arjun had no idea of what she looked like, and wasn't going to point her out. Arjun wasn't looking where he was going and collided into Gorbind's shoulder.

"There," he told Arjun, having finally espied Padmi at twelve minutes passed three. Holding onto Arjun's shoulder, Gorbind swivelled him around on his heels. "Go introduce yourself," he said nudging him along.

"What?" Arjun half squawked. "But she doesn't know me from Adam!" he protested, his face was starting to pull against gravity.

"Shift," hissed Gorbind, shoving Arjun further forward and he himself peeled off towards the bar. He waited there, shuffling along the queue of three others ahead of him. Gorbind casually glanced over his shoulder whilst he waited.

Arjun and Padmi had found each other. They had a few more minutes to exchange pleasantries before he would join them.

Gorbind was eventually served and made his way through the dining area. He was the designated driver, so his drink was a pint of fizzy cola. If it all went pear-shaped, he would have to drown his sorrows later. Arjun's rather dark ale was sat before him onto a beer mat.

Padmi nodded appreciatively towards a glass of full-bodied Chilean Merlot placed in front of her.

"I like her!" declared Arjun, lifting his ale. "She's got two eyes, two ears; she didn't hit me when I asked to join her," he grinned as he took a hearty slug. "Apparently, she's heard a lot about me. I'm bang on the money about you driving like an old man. There's no danger of you ever being an F1 driver."

Laughter followed as all three of them clinked their glasses.

After, Padmi was giggling as she held her glass close. She grinned at Arjun, her one brow arched. "According to Gorbind, you pair went to Spain for your 21st. What's this about a sombrero, a stripper and a dodgy bit of tapas?" Padmi glanced briefly at Gorbind.

He had gone slightly pink at the mention of the sombrero.

Gorbind nodded at Arjun, before sipping his fizzy drink.

Arjun frowned, as though expecting a defensive tirade. Not getting one. He shuffled closer to Padmi.

"Let's start with the tapas," he giggled wryly. "That's probably the cleanest bit to be honest," Arjun's eyes were startling to glint with mischief. "We can work backwards towards the sombrero."

The Spanish narrative took another twenty minutes to unravel; each and every thread was untangled in detail. Gorbind let the two of them talk; he sat observing whilst drinking his cola. There was no reason to interject, to comment or clarify. What he wanted to do, was make sure that they could sit together; make sure that they had something to join them.

He needed to know that two of his favourite people could breathe the same air and not kill each other.

"You know you're the first," Arjun sighed contentedly, moving his hand to curl his digits around Padmi's. "The first girlfriend of his, that I've met," there was a momentary sideling glance at Gorbind. "You're not just run of the mill special; you must be more than special."

Feeling his cheeks flush, Gorbind caught Padmi's gaze trained upon him. Her brows were arched somewhat.

"I must be," she said smirking. "He's meeting my

parents soon," Padmi tipped him the wink. "Guess he's a bit special too. Then there's you granny, Arjun," she said turning back to face him.

"Nani," Gorbind finally interjected. His throat had felt clammed shut whilst watching and listening to them talk.

"Really?" Arjun's interest had piqued; he shuffled a little closer to elbow Gorbind. "She is really special, proper special," he said waggling a finger at Gorbind. "This one you keep. This one, I want to adopt, make friends with, and call my own. Tell Nani I said so."

"Thank you, little brother, for your seal of approval," Gorbind nodded at Padmi, lifting his drink to slurp noisily. "I shall keep that in mind."

"A pleasure." Arum drummed his fingers as his smile became a fixed grin. "Calls for another drink, my round, me thinks." Up he rose and headed towards the bar.

Sliding across into Arjun's seat, Padmi moved close enough to kiss Gorbind.

He could taste the bitter cherry in her merlot, and was rather sorry to be staying sober. The kiss itself was wildly intoxicating. The Chilean Merlot might as well have been negligible.

"He's cute," she said softly, a smile dancing across her

lips to dimple her cheeks. He'd never noticed that happen before.

"Reckon you could cope with him," queried Gorbind. "Sometimes, he's as mad as a box of frogs. Beyond that, Padmi, he's my baby brother and the world's best wing-man. If you want me, you'll have to tolerate him. If he were to annoy you, I would clip his wings, I promise."

Shaking her head, Padmi rubbed the apples of his cheeks with her thumbs. "Don't worry about that," she said, her lashes fluttering. "No danger of Arjun annoying me. Your wing-man means the world to you, he will mean no less to me. Your baby brother is my baby brother; it's that simple."

Neither one of them noticed Arjun return.

Gorbind was lost; he was too far gone in Padmi's eyes to register anything.

It was only when Arjun coughed pointedly that he and Padmi parted from their embrace. Arjun put another round of drinks down onto the table.

As he made a start in a second pint of cola, he felt a greater sense of relief. Padmi and Arjun would be fine; all he had to do was get through meeting her parents. Padmi meeting Nani would be the next big thing after that.

Feeling bubbles burst upon the edges of his tongue, he watched Padmi and Arjun twitter. They were talking as though they were long lost friends.

All would hopefully end well.

He didn't care what came next. With Padmi by his side, nothing was insurmountable.

Nothing was beyond his grasp.

CHAPTER 3

"I brought Jalebis," Gorbind raised his arm aloft. A blue carrier bag dangled from his wrist. "You said your Dad likes them." In his other hand, there was a bouquet of carnations in different shades of pink.

Padmi rolled eyes her having clamped her arms around his waist. "Loves them," she pronounced, "His diabetes on the other hand," tutting loudly, she tugged his shirt to draw him over the threshold, down the hall and into the living room.

"Dad, it's Gorbind," she declared pushing the door open.

Gorbind saw Padmi's father stand up from the sofa. There was a television in the corner; the volume was reduced so that the football wouldn't interrupt proceedings.

"At last," exclaimed Subash, extending a hand towards Gorbind. "Gorbind, lovely to finally meet you. Please, come in, make yourself at home."

Handing Padmi the flowers, Gorbind shook her father's hand and held out the bag containing Jalebis.

"Jalebis, eh?" laughed Subash, "I heard you at the door. "Just don't tell my GP, or my wife for that matter."

As if on cue, a second woman appeared from behind a door at the other side of the room. Gorbind caught a glimpse of a galley kitchen, a stack of floral plates and a mound of crispy samosas.

Padmi waved at her mother.

"Oh, no," Subash looked at the T.V., and tutted. "Why is it that every time Blues play city, they get thumped sideways."

"Dodgy defence," commented Gorbind. He tracked ticker tape that travelled across the bottom of the large, curved, plasma screen. "No money to buy a new one."

"Tell me about it," nodded Subash, "Here take a seat," he said sitting back onto the sofa, and patted the space next to him.

Gorbind did as he was told, he looked at Padmi with some degree of triumph. Football was not only a beautiful game, the language was universal.

"Bluenose?" Subash asked, picking up a remote.

"Villain," coughed Gorbind, a fist curled before his mouth as he looked Padmi's father in the eye.

Padmi appeared to freeze, stopping as she approached the kitchen door.

For a moment, Gorbind and Subash eyeballed each other.

"Lapsed," Gorbined ventured tentatively. "Play offs and relegation make it hard to keep the faith. But you got to keep right on, eh."

"Keep right on," nodded Subash, laughing quietly. "I live in hope. We'll make a bluenose of you yet. But first, tea! Er, Padmi...."

Padmi darted off, she didn't need telling twice.

Gorbind caught her sigh in relief. She'd mentioned in passing that she came from a family of Bluenoses; that her father knew the city divides well and took them very seriously. In this part of the world, football and postal codes had an interesting relationship. Your footballing allegiance was determined by how far your place of birth was from the nearest stadium.

"Midlands aside," said Gorbind, wanting to test the boundaries further. "I took Arjun to the Cup Final last year."

"Chelsea versus Arsenal?" Subash took his eyes of the T.V. for two tenths of a second.

"One hell of a game," Gorbind commented. "Fortress Wembley is a sight to be seen."

For fifteen minutes, Gorbind made the best footballing small talk that he could muster. Arjun had briefed him about the safe areas. Not only was Gorbind a lapsed Villain, he was also a decade behind most people. His quip about a dodgy defence was a shot from the distant past and a massive fluke.

When Padmi arrived with a tray of tea, Gorbind felt his own defences slip and relax a little. He had waffled for England and then some. Padmi's mum followed, she had crockery and a pile of delicious looking samosas.

Putting down the tray, Padmi sat next to him on the sofa. She formed a barrier between him and Subash as she handed over tea and samosas.

Gorbind could smell the headiness of the spices in the tea; there were very specific notes of cardamom and cinnamon. The scent was wonderfully soothing, all things considered.

What ever happened next, he had tea and samosas.

CHAPTER 4

Sometime later and stuffed to the gills, Gorbind stepped out the front door to stand on the drive.

Not only was his stomach crammed with samosas and sweets, but his head was also starting to spin somewhat.

"Well, that was interesting," he said, zipping up his cagoule over a pale pink shirt that matched his dark blue jeans. "Was that the plan?" Gorbind asked. He looked up to see Padmi close the front door behind her and lean against it. "To stuff me and your dad with tea and samosas; I'd comply, be putty in his hands. He'd be too full to ask my intentions, unable to kneecap me with your brother's hockey stick."

Crossing her arms, Padmi smiled as her eyelashes

fluttered. "Did it work?" she asked, her grin beaming at him.

Gorbind bent to check where his knees were. "I've still got them," he said laughing. "I'm not in a puddle on the floor. My intentions weren't questioned." Straightening up, he shuffled into Padmi's arms.

Some part of him felt like he was sailing close to the wind; her parents were only yards away behind the door. He could hear the clink and clatter of crockery being cleared away.

"Are they still dishonourable?" she asked, pulling him closer.

"Completely," he replied, looming in to kiss her. "Will never be any other way," he added, once his lips had parted from hers. "Will you come see Nani at the weekend?" there was hopefulness in his tone. "Then everything really is above board. You've met Arjun; you didn't smack him, so that's a good thing, I guess." He was however, distracted whist trying to pull his car keys from his pocket.

"He's lovely," trilled Padmi, pulling him back to cradle his face in her palms. "I'll come see Nani, yes," she traced a finger across his cheekbone and towards his lips. "Otherwise, it's Goodnight Vienna. Without Nani and I meeting, this won't get very far now, will it?"

Gorbind silently shook his head whilst looking at his feet.

"Exactly," Padmi continued. "I'll bring a plant, some barfi too. Say I arrive in time for lunch. We can see if I make it til tea time?"

Nodding, Gorbind took her palm into his. "Agreed," he said quietly. "This will be okay, won't it?" he planted her palm over his fast-beating heart. "I don't know what I'll do, if she doesn't approve."

Padmi's gaze travelled to where he had put her hand. Her hand pressed firmer against his jacket.

Gorbind gulped, his heart was racing far more than it had been when he had first arrived over two hours ago.

"Does it worry you that much?" Padmi whispered.

"Terrifies me," uttered Gorbind, trying to keep his tone from wavering. "I don't want to break your heart, if Nani breaks mine."

"She won't," Padmi lurched forward; there was a tessellation of curves and contours as she threw her arms around him. Gorbind was almost winded by the impact; then there was how tightly she held on. This wasn't a delicate hug, this was deep rooted enough to almost knock him from his feet.

All he had to do, was have faith; he had to believe

that Nani would approve.

Anything else really didn't bear thinking about.

CHAPTER 5

"You can eat these, you know," Nani quickly unwrapped the Aloe Vera plant that Padmi had walked in with. "Some people, take a leaf," she said running a finger down the side of one, "Grate it and put it into rotis. Thank you," Nani smiled, before shuffling away to put it in pride of place in the middle of the kitchen window.

Nani's kitchen was where he and Padmi had been ushered into on arrival. With the three of them standing in middle, it felt altogether crowded.

"Shall I put the kettle on?" offered Gorbind. "Padmi brought barfi too," he glanced over his shoulder as Padmi waggled a red and white, striped carrier bag.

"You do that, yes," nodded Nani, tapping his elbow.

Picking up a plate from the drainer, Nani took Padmi by the hand. "You come with me, Beta. I've trained him well," she smiled, dimpling her doughy cheeks. "Let's see if he actually took anything in."

"PADMI!" Arjun effectively screamed the house down as he frantically trundled down the stairs. He then almost collided with the two women in the hallway.

"Hey!" Padmi's response wasn't nearly as high-pitched as she was engulfed in Arjun's wide-armed bear hug.

Nani intervened quickly, jabbing Arjun in the back. "You go help your brother make tea, let me speak with Padmi," she said, shepherding her away.

"Divide and conquer," Arjun told Gorbind. "Listen," he said edging into the kitchen. "Just listen to what Nani says; this could be one hell of an interrogation." Arjun waggled his eyebrows as the lounge door being left wide open. "I'll do the tea," he said shooing Gorbind away. "You eavesdrop as discretely as you can."

Squinting at Arjun, Gorbind knew he was right. He edged forwards to hover between the living room and the kitchen.

"Your Mum and Dad, they always lived here?" Nani was starting gently.

He was doing his best to imagine who was sat where. From his vantage point, all he could see was an elbow.

"My mum was born here," he heard Padmi say. "My dad was born in Kenya. All of my grandparents came over in the late sixties."

"That's when we all came over," he could imagine Nani nodding with nostalgia. "Better life for our children," she added. Gorbind could hear wistfulness in her words.

He continued to listen. Over the next ten minutes, the conversation was fairly innocuous and bordered on inane. Ten minutes was enough for Arjun to be a pseudo-domestic God and make tea.

It was however, Gorbind's job to take it into the living room. From what he had heard so far, he felt that Padmi had held her own.

"I've got a younger brother too," Padmi scooted over as Arjun joined her alongside Nani. "So I know how one of these works," she said winking at him.

"This one is special," Nani poked playfully poked her younger grandson. "Full scale drama-walla. Drama Queen, that's what he calls himself."

Gorbind caught Padmi's gaze as he felt into an armchair. He had mentioned it in anticipation, very briefly. When they'd met, Arjun had filled Padmi in with all the relevant bits and pieces. There was a whole story about how Arjun had come out. His grandmother had barely batted an eyelid when both and Arjun had expected her to blow several culturally-bound gaskets.

"You just worry about that one," Nani pointed directly at him. "He can make roti, dahl, and sabji too. Him, I trained properly.

"I burn most things," Arjun piped up, not sounding in the least bit apologetic as he shrugged. "I can make tea, though."

"Gorbind will look after you," Nani put her hand to Padmi's knee. "You'll look after each other, hopefully. He talks about you all the time. Padmi this, Padmi that. Tell me about this Mattar Paneer."

"Nani, no," Gorbind felt his stomach flip at the mention of the dish; he shifted uneasily in his seat. Pressing his palms to his face, he knew that he was going deep red. "Don't mention the Mattar Paneer."

"Sugar, not salt," Padmi laughed as she clapped her palms together. "Then it all boiled dry; we forgot about it as we…."

Gorbind's eyes were wide as she stopped short; they both knew why she had stopped short. It wasn't the sort of thing to disclose to your granny. They exchanged rather pointed looks; a silent acknowledgment not to go any further.

"What you made me today, Gorbind?" Padmi asked, changing tact. "As you're so well trained."

"A big mess!" Nani declared, her bangles jangled as she laughed heartily. "Gobi, yellow dahl," she added, once more tapping Padmi's knee. "He took my kitchen over completely; wouldn't let me in at all. That makes you special, Beta," Nani looked at Gorbind and waggled a finger at him. "If you're special to him, then that makes you special to me. I'm glad that you found him, that you agreed to come see me. You've brought sunshine here today, Padmi, and that's means more to me than I can say."

And there it was; Nani's seal of approval.

Gorbind was fixed into his seat at Nani engulfed Padmi in a big hug. The sound of Ajun whooping wasn't enough to break the thrall.

He had Padmi, he had sunshine. Gorbind's world was not only that much more solid, it was also a hell of a lot brighter.

CHAPTER 6

"Gorbind, pick up your damned 'phone. Nani's not well."

Dropping his lunch onto his desk, Gorbind heard his brother's voice message. Arjun's panicked sharp tone immediately ramped up his anxiety. Gorbind had missed six calls, seven messages and two other voice messages.

This did not bode well.

Grabbing his coat and keys, he poked his head around the door of his manager's office.

"I gotta go, family emergency. Gran's been taken ill, will report in as soon as," his words sped out. The brunette behind the desk looked at him with her mouth agape; her 'phone pressed to her ear. That probably wasn't the best thing to do. He had only been in post three weeks; his finals had only just come and gone. Fever-Newton Statistics had taken him on in good faith when he didn't officially graduate for a few more weeks.

Gorbind ran. He ran down four flights of stairs, across a crowded, congested car park and into his car. Sliding his 'phone into a cradle on the dash, he listened to all of Arjun's frenzied messages.

"Nani's not well," Arjun had said in the first message. "Chest pains, shortness of breath. I've called an ambulance."

Speeding out of the car park, Gorbind joined traffic that traversed the city.

"We're in the ambulance," Arjun sounded grave in the next message. "It's definitely a heart attack. We're headed to the QE. Get there, ASAP. I'm scared. Nani's scared too. I've called Padmi; Nani was asking for her. Get here."

As he continued to drive, he saw Padmi's name flash on his 'phone from the corner of his eye. Thankfully, the device was connected to the car's dash.

"Gorbind?" Padmi was rasping on the other end of the line. "Are you on the way? I'm two minutes away. I'll probably find Arjun before you do."

"Okay," Gorbind struggled to speak, his throat was dry and his heart was beating so hard he could hear it. "Look after them, Padmi. I'll get there as soon as I can."

"I will," agreed Padmi. "Drive safely. I'll hold the fort. Love you."

"You too," Gorbind just about got his words out. His chest was feeling heavy and had become tight. It hurt to breathe. He half put his foot down as he joined a dual-carriage way.

If anything happened to Nani whilst he wasn't there, he really wouldn't forgive himself.

Gorbind felt horribly dizzy having negotiated the hospital's multi-story car park. He parked at one of the upper most levels to then sprint across the site to accident and emergency. In his head, all sorts of scenarios played out.

Had Nani been alone, where had Arjun been, would she survive and was she still in pain?

Each scenario built up; every permutation became heavier and harder to process. There was no part of him that could imagine Nani not being part of his world. This was a thought that really didn't bear thinking about; a thought, that for years, he and Arjun had point blank refused to discuss.

Breathless and disorientated, Gorbind arrived at A&E.

"Gurmukh Kaur Hayer," he told the receptionist. He tried to focus, tried get his breath back whilst staying up right. There was a small danger that he might end up in a heap on the floor. He really didn't want to end up on a trolley. That would only give Padmi and Arjun something unnecessary to worry about.

Fiddling for what felt like an eternity, the receptionist eventually found Nani's information on his computer. It took another two minutes for Gorbind to find out where he had to go as well as how to get there. His head bulged with directions. He staggered and swayed as he followed them. Eventually, Gorbind got to the curtained bay having negotiated a rabbit's warren of blue-linoleum floored corridors.

"Thank God!" exclaimed Arjun. He hurtled towards Gorbind with his arms stretched out. The hug kept Gorbind upright, but he wasn't about to confess that right there and then.

Gorbind held onto Arjun for a good few minutes. The both of them were shaking almost violently.

"It's okay," he told Arjun, his hands clamped onto his brother's shoulders. Shoulders that really shouldn't haven't carried all of this alone. "Let's do this. Where is she?" he asked, surprised that he was able to string his words together.

"Here," Arjun peeled away a curtain. "Padmi got here too."

Nani looked grey; the same shade of grey that lead might be. That was what struck Gorbind as he immediately ran to her bedside.

She looked grey and scared.

He was scared too. He'd never felt so scared in his entire adult life.

Gorbind didn't even want to touch her, should she break and leave him.

Leave him, Padmi and Arjun.

His stomach flipped as Nani took his hand to pull him closer towards the trolley she was sat upon. From the corner of his eye, he saw Padmi prop up Arjun. His brother was perilously close to keeling over.

"Please don't leave me," he uttered. Gorbind spoke in Punjabj rather than in English. As though using another language would be more convincing. It tool every bit of linguistic nous that he could muster.

"Can't," replied Nani. "I want to watch you graduate, get married, have babies," she said quietly, "Both of you," she added, flicking a wrist at Arjun and with some effort. "I bought a new suit for your graduation;

Padmi helped me make it. I'm not going anywhere. No one is taking me just yet. This will all be fine, you don't need to worry, Beta. You don't need to worry at all."

But he did worry; Gorbind couldn't do anything else. He worried as Nani was prepped for a stent, worried as she came around and was in hospital for a week. He worried when he drove her home and didn't leave her for another two days.

This had been too close for comfort, too close to home. Nani was all that he had left, all that he left of his mum. Gorbind had been young when his mother had died. Losing Nani would be catastrophic; he just wasn't ready for that.

He doubted that he ever would be.

CHAPTER 7

As he rubbed his eyes with the heels of his palms, Gorbind watched Padmi drape a black and blue blanket across Arjun as he slept. He had fallen asleep after lunch and was thoroughly exhausted.

They all were.

Two days of making sure Nani was recovering had taken a toll on all of them.

"Let's go take a walk," Padmi told him as she glanced over her shoulder. "You need some fresh air. It's time to stand down for a bit, okay? Half an hour or so at The Mill Pond ought to do it."

Nodding, Gorbind conceded. He wasn't about to argue; he simply didn't have the energy.

He said nothing as they walked to The Mill Pond. The journey was a smidgeon under ten minutes. He and Padmi took a gentle amble along to the still working Mill that sat upon a parcel of lush green, wooded land and was a local heritage site. It was a little deserted today though. A couple of long-haired, fluffy-furred dogs were being walked by their owners. The pooches were in no rush to chase the local squirrels. In high summer, the whole place teemed with families. You couldn't move for picnic baskets and Frisbees that flew in every direction.

This was no ordinary walk in the park. The Mill Pond was special, another sanctuary. This was where he had told Padmi everything. He had told Padmi how he felt, how she was the centre of his universe.

How she was his whole world.

Padmi walked him through the entrance gate. His fingers were intertwined with hers in the pocket of her coat. Now was not the time to mention damp tissue and rustling sweet wrappers. He followed, basically at heel, through the square, brick building where tickets for the Mill could be bought. Gorbind was led across the courtyard and past the tearoom. There was a narrow pathway just left of the tearoom, and he glanced at the flower beds either side.

The beds gave way to a railed viewing platform. Here they both looked out across The Mill Pond. A couple of mallards sat serenely on the surface of the water.

"Breathe," said Padmi, taking his hand from her pocket and pulling his arm around her. "Just five minutes. Take this all in, let everything else go. It's all okay."

Gorbind curled his arm around her waist and shuffled to make sure she stood in the crook of his elbow. As ever, he was compliant; his shoulders sagged from on high. He resisted shifting his weight entirely onto her.

"Thank you," he whispered, pressing his head against hers.

"This is what we do," Padmi said gently. "When you love someone, when you need someone; you walk through their fire, through their storms as though they were your own. Never let them go."

He knew those words. Those words were very familiar.

"And I do love you," Padmi continued, turning slightly so that they were facing each other.

She was about to give him the speech.

His speech.

The one that he had practiced for days; the speech that had travelled from the bottom of his heart and the outer edges of his soul.

Gorbind bit his lip; edging forward, he encircled her waist with his arms. His elbows sat neatly against the curve of her hips.

"I love you, Gorbind," Padmi's mouth blossomed with a smile. This was a smile that accentuated the curve of Cupid's bow lips. "You are the sunshine that makes my world brighter. It's your smile that tells me all is okay. It's in your hands that I put my universe. It's for you that my heart beats; it's you that takes away my every breath. Without you, I am lost and alone. With you, I feel sheer bliss. Say you will be mine. That you feel for me, what I feel for you and I simply cannot put into words. You are my today, my tomorrow and my everything."

"Four years and you didn't forget," Gorbind struggled to get his words out, she had rather taken his breath away. "You got it all."

"Every single word is committed to memory," she replied. Shifting her weight, Padmi stood on the tip of her toes to close his mouth with a kiss.

She was right. Everything was okay. Today, tomorrow and forever.

CHAPTER 8

"Nani, just hold my hands," Arjun flexed his fingers towards his grandmother. "Hurry up, you two!" he whistled sharply as Gorbind came closer with Padmi hanging from his arm.

"I'm going to brain him," Gorbind commented through gritted teeth. Padmi gave his hand a squeeze, to calm him down a little. "My head hurts. Does he have to be so loud?"

"Everything's loud today," said Padmi, blinking several times in quick succession. "God only knows who suggested going out to celebrate graduation. Whoever they are, they need shooting. You do not know how much concealer it took to cover up the aftermath. Tequila should be made illegal."

"And the bourbon chasers," grimaced Gorbind. "Say nothing to Nani," he whispered, as they walked alongside towards the steps up the fountain in Victoria Square. Fellow graduands milled around the fountain and the council house. The Town Hall was similarly thronging with people in caps and gowns. Both he and Padmi were dressed in university colours, cap and gown.

Behind him, Padmi's parents and brother followed. Padmi peeled off to go speak with them; she adjusted the pins that held her mortar board in place above a tight, neatly-tied bun.

"Look at you," Nani let go of Arjun's hand to edge towards Gorbind. She was dressed in a crushed coral pink shalwar khameez dotted with silver sequins. "Here, you've got dust and all sorts on you," Nani swept away lint from his shoulders before pulling his gown tighter across his shoulders. "You look lovely in your suit," her cheeks dimpled as she squeezed his cheek. "Do you like mine?"

"I do," he replied. Gorbind couldn't help but beam back at her. She had fussed for weeks about what she would wear. This was the first graduation that she going to; this meant that the whole thing was buzzing with excitement.

"Two seconds!" yelled Arjun, pulling out his 'phone. "Nani say cheese," he waved his hand, directing

Gorbind to move. Sunshine had spontaneously appeared, playing havoc with photographs by making everything a bit sparkly.

Gorbind's grin couldn't have been broader as he posed with his grandmother. Nani's face was an absolute picture; she couldn't haven't smiled any more either. To think that only a few weeks ago, she had been seriously ill. She was only just the same colour as her outfit. Gorbind would never forget how ashen-grey she had looked in the hospital or the fear that had hung around them all as a family. A fear that was really quite palpable and lingered like a bum-note in the middle of a symphony.

"Come on then," Nani linked her arm his. "You two can both walk me up those stairs. She pulled a face at half-naked nymph that was depicted bathing in the fountain. It had been years since there had been any water involved. The fountain had been planted up with flowers after a rather expensive leak had been found. "Arjun, I need you too. Come here."

Arjun dutifully did as he was told to take up Nani's other arm.

Glancing over his shoulder, Gorbind silently checked in with Padmi. She nodded in return; they would see each other inside. Nani was their priority. She had been adamant that she would watch graduation, come hell, high water and heart attack.

Twenty minutes later, Gorbind took his seat in the hall. He looked up to the Gods and waved at Nani. Only *his* grandmother would wave back with a screwed up ball of kitchen roll gripped in her palm. As he processed down the aisle to receive his degree from the chancellor, Gorbind was convinced that the wild whooping that he heard was most definitely his Nani.

CHAPTER 9

His feet were cold. Clad in rather thin pink and blue striped socks, his feet didn't appreciate being exposed to a few degrees Celsius. The rest of Gorbind was comfortably cocooned within several layers of clothing. Padmi had reminded him several times to pack properly for their weekend away. He just hadn't fancied packing Grandad-esque thermal socks. He had made no bone about his dislike of Britain's wet, windy and downright miserable, festive weather. His foot curled as he untied the rented ice-skate to put them on. On Gorbind's head was a blue and white bobble hat that matched his puffy, quilted jacket.

"Come on, hurry up," Padmi urged as she too pulled on skates. She was sat a short distance away and was all too animated. The British Museum loomed over them as they sat on a bench; in its shadow was an ice-rink that appeared close to Christmas every year.

"Yes, dear," sighed Gorbind sliding down the bench to sit next to her. Letting out a spontaneous belch, he looked around a little abashed as he put two fingers to his lips. He'd lost count of how many bottled, blonde beers he had actually drank over lunch.

Padmi shook her head before sliding her feet together. "I don't mind the burping," she said, turning to face him a little. "Just don't go to sleep on ice because you ate too much."

"I did eat too much," stated Gorbind, tugging his laces tight to tie them. "I agree with that. I didn't pay for anything, you wouldn't let me. I took full advantage of everything. This is, after all, all your idea. A dirty weekend in London, doing with me as you wish." He felt his face flush hot as he caught Padmi's eye-line.

"And ice-skating; that's actually inspired," he couldn't help but nod in concession. "I'm rather impressed that you remembered." Lowering his gaze to his feet, Gorbind arched a brow. He had no idea how to do this. Ice-skating was all very romantic, but he never thought he would be doing it.

A throwaway comment made at Valentines, had come back to bite him.

Gorbind didn't have too long to dwell upon it. Padmi had linked her arm around his and pulled him to his feet. In tow, he had no choice to follow as she stomped her way towards the rink. He stomped too; he felt awkward and very much like a fish out of water. The water in question was entirely frozen and congested as people travelled across it in every direction.

"I aim to please," said Padmi, briefly looking at him over her shoulder and then back at the ice.

As he watched people move, Gorbind felt his gut grumble. A tight knot of anxiety twanged across his spleen. His one arm stretched out ahead; Padmi held his fingers in something of a vice-like grip. Fingers that were now very hot and sweaty. His other hand was curled around the rail around the rink, hanging on for dear life.

He really didn't want to step out onto the ice.

In his head, the fantasy of gliding across the ice with Padmi was all very fuzzy, all very romantic; the element of slush made him very warm inside. Given the bitter winter cold, that warmness was worth hanging onto for as long as physically possible.

However, there was noise, clamour; up ahead, someone had landed on their backside with all the grace of a malfunctioning torpedo.

Padmi had felt him resist, she looked at him over her shoulder. A veil of silken locks fell across her face. She pushed it all away with perfectly painted finger tips. "You can stand there and be chicken," she said rather loudly. "I'll tell Arjun all about it. Or you can get a wiggle; we can wibble-wobble along together." She tugged sharply at his arm. "I'll keep a hold of you, I promise," Padmi continued to stomp, flexing her fingers to increase the grip on his hand. "If you go down, I'll come with you. Arjun can then hear about us hitting the ice, how we did it together."

Lowering his head a little, Gorbind arched a brow. "Together?" he asked. "Us two falling together is better than just me landing on my backside, when it comes to my brother taking the rise?"

Padmi made no verbal answer; instead, she tugged harder at his arm.

Gorbind felt himself being propelled forward, at speed too. His face blanched with the prospect of nose-diving onto ice. Rather than falling flat, he was all arms and legs. Padmi moved nimbly on her blades to get a grip of his forearms, then his elbows to keep him upright. His hands grasped the woolly fabric of her coat. For the moment, Gorbind was still standing; he was however, quaking in his girlfriend's arms.

"Hey, sshh, it's okay." Padmi held onto his arms tightly. "We're both still upright," she said quietly.

"No one's going to hit the deck just yet." Padmi moved her blades to position her feet either side of his. "Your backside is in perfectly safe hands," she smirked as her hands moved to the aforementioned derriere. "Let's see how this goes, we can take this really slowly."

"No Bolero?" whispered Gorbind, his nose millimetres from Padmi's. "Or any other bump and grind to be done on the ice."

Rolling her eyes, Padmi shuffled aside. Taking both of his hands into hers, she edged backwards to get them both into motion.

Gorbind made no moan. He was being carried away, and he rather liked it. Padmi had him in her hands; there was no place he would rather be. Plus, she had given him her word. If he went down, she was going with him.

The next hour or so was spent being pushed, pulled and even twirled around. Gorbind laughed, screamed, he landed on his backside a few times. Each time, Padmi had stretched out her hand to pull him back to his feet. Each time, she had checked for any dents and damage. It was only when the evening air became icy, when he could see her breath hang in the air, that he mentioned making a retreat for dinner.

Gorbind followed Padmi off the ice. Once more, he

let himself be carried away.

"See it's all in one piece," her face crinkled with glee.

He was caught off guard once again, as Padmi familiarised herself with the curve of his rear end.

"It's probably a bit bruised," Padmi continued, "I suspect it might be a bit blue in places.

Safely off the rink, Gorbind took great pleasure in pulling Padmi into his arms. "It all yours," he was unable to suppress laughter whilst their foreheads pressed together. "To do with, as you wish."

Padmi grinned back; she passed the tip of her tongue across her lip before biting it coquettishly. "Careful what you wish for, Gorbind Phalla. This could be one hell of a weekend."

CHAPTER 10

Every now and again, Gorbind flexed his ankle and dropped his foot to the rubber mat in the foot-well. Had he been in the driving seat, this reflex would've see him breaking to moderate his speed. As he was in the passenger seat of Padmi's compact Toyota, Gorbind was uncomfortable. The speeding was one thing, but he also had to cope with a lack of leg room. He was sat awkwardly, with his back to the driver in question and one hand on the handle above his head as he held on for dear life.

This was not a pleasant experience.

"It wouldn't kill you, to slow down," he grumbled. Gorbind momentarily gulped down the rapidly rising contents of an unsettled stomach. "We're not in a hurry. Plus, we didn't have to leave so early." He had tried to sleep over the last two hours. However, the journey had felt far from smooth and there was still another two hours to go. He really disliked not being in the driving seat.

Padmi shook her head, not taking her eyes off the road,

He saw her eyelashes flutter from behind the lenses of her oversized, designer sunglasses. The sun was starting to fill the sky to better illuminate their route towards Brighton. Having sunglasses on at this time of the day made no sense to him whatsoever.

"If you and Arjun hadn't drunk so much, you'd be alright," she said, fiddling with the air conditioning and directing a vent towards him.

A cold pulse of air hit him squarely on the jaw. Gorbind shuffled around as he tried to get more comfortable and tugged at his seat belt.

"Didn't drink that much," he muttered. "Just forgot to eat before-hand. We've brought snacks, yes?" he asked, catching sight of a blue carrier bag that was nestled beside his feet. There was also a thermos flask sitting on its side.

"Nani packed you parathas," replied Padmi, as she flicked the indicator stalk to smoothly change lanes.

Hauling the bag into his lap, Gorbind rummaged

inside. There were a couple of bottles of water, a stash of chocolate bars and a sharing bag of crisps. Last by not least, he found a lumpy, aluminium foil package that barely contained the scent of spiced potatoes. Cumin; Gorbind recognised the unforgettable scent of cumin. As he unwrapped the shiny foil, he then had to get passed sheets of kitchen roll that were spotted with ghee and a multi-coloured duck motif.

Gorbind counted the stack the stack of stuffed chappatis. "Six," he said, turning a little towards Padmi. "Apparently, Nani expects us to eat six parathas between us."

"I'd eat three," nodded Padmi, her lips parting into a pearly-white smile that caught the sun. "Nani makes awesome parathas."

"The sort that send you into a food coma," Gorbind chuckled as he folded one into halves and tore it down the middle.

"The sort that are filled with love, Gorbind," said Padmi, her hand drifted from the wheel and towards the halved paratha. "Give me a bit; tear some off for me."

Doing as he was told, Gorbind pinched off a tiny, flaky, ghee-imbued morsel and dropped it into Padmi's palm.

No sooner had it dropped into her palm, Padmi lifted it away. Cupping her fingers, she tossed the morsel into her mouth.

"Should I ask?" posed Gorbind, "What we're doing, beside the seaside, and whether or not I should worry? God forbid, you drag me to the beach for a 'here to eternity' moment."

Padmi gave something of a dry laugh; her eyes flicked briefly towards him from the road. "That would be rather interesting, what with all the shingle in your creases," she even smirked a little. "Just relax," she added gently.

"Shingle?" he tutted. Gorbind carried on tearing his paratha into pieces, this time for himself. "I just want to know what you plan to do with me exactly. Have this weekend free, she said. You, me, sea, sand and stuff, she promised. Don't call this a dirty weekend, Gorbind," he narrowed his eyes, wondering if Padmi was rise to his mimicry.

"Give me some more paratha please," she said, putting out her palm once more. "I lied. If this isn't a dirt weekend, I will be sorely disappointed."

Gorbind's ears pricked up, his stomach forgot that it was unsettled. His gut actually fizzled with excitement instead. "No disappointment then," he said, handing over bits of paratha, "Do with me as you wish, I shall comply."

CHAPTER 11

Bleary-eyed, Gorbind opened the curtains a smidgeon. He peered through the gap and winced. A huge, yellow ball of fire was suspended across an endless panel of blue. Below the skyline, water sparkled and shimmered as it rippled towards the shore and back. On the far left of the vista, Brighton Pier jutted out into the sea. At the end of the pier, a Ferris wheel span slowly.

From the sea-front hotel, he could see bodies bob and bounce across shingle that was strewn with brightly coloured beach towels. The weather forecast for the weekend had been freakishly good for the middle of British summertime. People were quite rightly making the most of it. Warm weather in Blighty didn't tend to happen very often, or last that long for that matter.

He wanted to enjoy it too.

Being by the seaside was wonderfully therapeutic. As children, he and Arjun had made several trips to Skegness with Aunty Leela. Donkey ride and home-made picnics had always been a big part of the annual family day-trip. To this day, there was something strangely soothing and wonderfully hypnotic about being sat on the sand watching the sea caress the sand as it ebbed back and forth.

The rolling tide stirred his soul and helped Gorbind feel an almost ethereal sense of peace.

The sort of peace that money couldn't buy and only love could help you appreciate.

Gorbind drew back the curtains to let out a deep, all-encompassing yawn. The early start had caught up with him; it had caught up with them both. Feeling tiredness tug at his every limb, he yawned widely whilst he stretched his arms out. He padded back towards a mound of white duvet that was heaped upon a double bed.

"Are you coming back in?" a hand snaked out from below the heap as Gorbind sat down next to it.

It didn't take long before Padmi pulled him in and back under the mound.

"It's really beautiful outside," Gorbind half-heartedly protested. "Sun's out and everything," he added, unable to resist as Padmi pulled him closer towards the centre of the heaped duvet.

"Out there, the shingle would hurt," said Padmi, her fingers had already made short work of removing his boxers. "Being here is far more comfortable."

Conceding defeat, Gorbind forgot about the sunshine.

He had a whole weekend. With any luck, it would stick around.

CHAPTER 12

Sunshine on a Saturday felt more special compared to any other day. Especially when enjoyed with an ice-cream and a pint at the seaside. Taking a mouthful of cold, crisp, extremely blonde lager, Gorbind savoured it with this soul. His ice-cream was in a small plastic bowl and starting to form a puddle dotted with brightly-coloured sugar strands.

"How are the feet, champ?" asked Padmi, peering over the large ovals of her sunglasses. "Sore?"

"A little," he said glancing down at the chestnut-coloured sandals that Padmi had insisted he bring with him. He had purchased them under duress too. So far, the footwear had proved to be really quite useful. She had dragged him almost everywhere around Brighton. There had been the lanes, the Pavilion and this afternoon, the shore. "But your shoulders are far worse," he said, pointing at the splodges of red that were visible either side of bright orange spaghetti straps.

Padmi looked at him confused; her brows had knitted tightly together. She momentarily pursed her lips together before looking at each shoulder in turn. "Oww," she grimaced, having surveyed the damage. "Didn't realise; didn't think I need sunscreen. This is Britain after all, not Fuerta Ventura."

Reaching into a pink and white striped beach-bag that was sat next to his feet, Gorbind took out a bottle of sunscreen. "Rule nothing out," he said opening the bottle as he got out of his seat. "I do have my uses," he said squirting some of the sunscreen into his hand. He gave the bottle to Padmi to stand behind her.

"You are becoming wonderfully well trained," Padmi closed her eyes as Gorbind followed the curve of her shoulders to slowly, systematically, apply sunscreen. Padmi's burned bits felt as though they were radiating hurt towards his fingers.

"I like every inch of you, you see," Gorbind had bent slightly to whisper into her ear. "And I'd rather there weren't any burned bits. I'd look after them though. I'd look after every part of you." He'd finished slathering on sun protection. Sliding his arm around her shoulder, he kissed the top of her head.

"Would you really?" she asked, holding his one had as he sat next to her again. "Look after me, every single bit?"

Gorbind picked up his melting ice-cream and the red spatula that it had come with. Scooping some up, he felt the coolness tingle on the tip of his tongue. "Every part," he said looking at her directly, "From your crispy shoulders, your just the right sized curves in all the right paces, to your knobbly knees that look like they are smiling and your right baby toe that lost its nail years ago."

"All of it?" Padmi asked again, she looked very much as though she was about to pounce. Her fingers twitched; twitched as though poised to spring her from the confines of her shiny, metal chair.

Gorbind nodded as he continued to eat his ice-cream. He was that engrossed that he missed Padmi launching herself towards him. With his feet just about planted onto the ground, his lap was swiftly occupied. His ice-cream was removed from him, thrown towards his pint as Padmi coiled around him.

"Always? Tell me that you will do that always, Gorbind?" Padmi unfastened herself to cradle his face in her hands. He could hear the anxiety in her voice, but also feel it vibrate as her ribcage collided with his.

Pulling her closer still, Gorbind anchored Padmi in place.

"Always," he said, nudging her nose. "Now, as we border on thirty. Then, we when have loads of kids, a dog and a white picket fence. Later still, when you are eighty-three, hard of hearing, yet tell me I sound like a sea-gull when I sleep."

"Cat," said Padmi, letting out breath. "We would have a cat."

"All right, a cat," he conceded with an eye roll. "A fluffy black one," he added, kissing a sunburned shoulder.

"You won't ditch me, upgrade me for a blonde," Padmi gently brought his face back towards her. "Red head, maybe?"

"Never in a million years," he replied. "I want you, and only you. Sunburned and all."

They sat for a while, drank cocktails whilst seeing the sun go down. Arm in arm, they walked back to the hotel. It was nine o' clock before he had listened to the dreams of hypothetical children. Gorbind posted his ticket on having two. He had become hungry, and curtailed the conversation by ordering Pizza. Padmi had whipped out two bottles of wine that had somehow remained chilled in her suitcase.

At three in the morning as Padmi slept with her head on shoulder, Gorbind watched her sleep as he endured a very sore head. He was too busy thinking about the hypothetical black cat.

He despised cats.

Padmi was the one. As long as he had her, he could deal with a hypothetical black cat.

CHAPTER 13

"Fish Tank?" Padmi asked; she looked at Gorbind through narrowed eyes. "You brought me to a fish tank on a date, is there some kind of subtext here?" she raised her eyebrows whilst wrapping two arms around his. "That maybe you're something of a cold fish to kiss."

Gorbind gave a slightly lopsided smirk as he side-stepped them both passed a little girl. A little girl dressed in purple, who whilst attached to reins was toddling excitedly towards a cavern ahead. What had her almost running was a group of small, squat penguins slicing in and out of icy blue water.

"You've not complained about the kissing so far," commented Gorbind. "You did say, you asked. Gorbind, can we do something different," he half squawked, affecting the slightly clipped at the edges accent that Padmi used on the 'phone. "We can always go to dinner, and no, I'm not spending two hours in the dark with you, watching a bad bloke movie-ow!" He was cut off sharply; Gorbind winced as he felt the pointed end of Padmi's elbow impact across his ribs.

He only just heard Padmi mutter the word 'fine' under her breath. Her grip on his arm got somewhat tighter; any tighter at his bicep and she could probably take his blood pressure. Gorbind enjoyed having Padmi close; feeling the warmth of her body heat was a bonus. They had been caught in a rather unexpected, very spontaneous downpour whilst walking through town. His coat was damp, heavy and absorbed every single joule of energy that Padmi radiated towards his skin.

"This, my darling, is different," he said pulling himself together a little. "Brave the fish for now," Gorbind chuckled quietly. "You can have lunch where ever you wish, I will not complain. Here, look, penguins," shifting his hands from the depths of his pockets, he used them both to hold hers. Her hands were freezing and had turned almost white. Gorbind pouted to pull a face before rubbing his palms rapidly across her hands to get the blood flowing properly.

"I know," bristling a little as she spoke, Padmi bit her lip. "The gloves that you gave me, are somewhere in my pocket. Just couldn't be asked to wear them. Oh, look, penguin!" she broke off her gaze; it was framed by fluttering, curved eyelashes to head towards the cavern. "Not small and fluffy are they? Not one bit. Gentoo penguins," she pronounced, reading a sign nearby.

Gorbind had to tilt his head to the right slightly and crane his neck a little to hear her. As adults, they stood quite literally head and shoulders above a newly-arrived, swarm of primary school children. The children filled the narrow galley of the Penguin cavern with hubbub, childish glee and infectious curiosity. All of which made it difficult for Gorbind to hang on Padmi's every word.

He was transfixed by the penguins; Gorbind watched the creatures intently. There were large rotund ones, with barrel-shaped bellies that lurching side to side as the birds moved. Barrel-shaped bellies that appeared to magically disappear as the birds plunged into a pool. In the water, they became swallow-like smudges cutting through swiftly. A couple of smaller, more slender shaped birds wandered across a ledge to greet the school children through viewing glass.

"Penguins are made of liquorice and almonds," said Padmi. "Covered in petroleum jelly, they don't break up and shatter when they hit the water. Mother Nature is weird and wonderful like that."

Penguins were made of liquorice. That was all he heard; that was all Gorbind registered as he snapped his head towards Padmi. "Liquorice?" he asked; his eyes wide. It took a moment as Gorbind shook his head in disbelief to come back into the room.

In that brief pocket of time, he had lost himself completely. He had been thinking about something else other than the penguins. Gorbind had been thinking about Ryton. He had to tell her, tell her what he had done. He also had to tell Nani too at some point.

"Where did you go exactly?" asked Padmi, she freed a hand to plant it gently on his jaw. "As pretty as the penguins are, you don't really come across as a bird-fancier."

Gorbind's shoulders dropped a little, he relaxed somewhat as she made light of his thoughts beyond the here and now. "Not these birds, no," he said, a smile dimpled his cheeks. "There's something I need to tell you," he said, edging them away from the artic and towards the central zone.

Traipsing ahead, he led Padmi out of the melee of kids that surrounded them. When he felt the tug, the resistance of her hand, he was pulled to a stop. Gorbind glanced over his shoulder to catch her lashes mid-flutter, her eyes zooming wide. Her gaze bored straight through him; Padmi's expression was altogether stormy and curious in equal measure.

He could feel the warmth of her fingers against his. She was gripping on hard, increasing the clamminess that felt like a film across his skin.

"You dare dump me in a fish tank, Gorbind Phalla," uttered Padmi. Her lips pursed together, emphasising a raspberry-kiss coated Cupid's bow. "Plus, it's Valentine's tomorrow. You do this, and I swear to God; you will rue the day that you were born." Her tone had risen, her words had been spat out with venom; she snatched back her hand. Padmi stood before him, her arms crossed and looking like the Mother Goddess enraged.

Gorbind had recoiled somewhat too. His feet were suddenly leaden, making him feel rooted to the spot. His ears were ringing too, having been boxed by Padmi's words. The ringing clashed horribly with the thudding of his heart. That was probably where all his blood had gone; his face felt numb whilst being fixed in shock.

"Don't do this," Padmi squeaked, shaking her head. She blinked a few times. Her eyes had glossed over with sheen of tears forming in abundance. Padmi licked the corner of her mouth, and he saw her chest rise and fall with letting out a sharp breath. Uncrossing her arms, she delicately passed two fingers across her lower lash line and flicked way two tears.

Gorbind saw the droplets fly through the air.

Tears, she was in tears. He had done this; he had made her cry. Of all the things to do to her, this tore his heart straight down the middle. Scampering towards her, Gorbind drew in breath. He curled his fingers to cup her shoulders; the damp fabric of her coat filled his palms.

"I'm not going to dump you."

"No?" sniffed Padmi, taking staccato breaths.

"No," replied Gorbind, wiping away mascara-tinged tears that were headed towards Padmi's lips. "Why would I dump you? I'm living day to day- hoping to High Heaven-that you, Padmi, don't flaming well dump me, for crying out loud."

"What else you got to say to me then?" Padmi's question was punctuated by a sniff and he felt her shoulders rise in anticipation.

"That I've applied to become a Police Officer," he let the words tumble out as he caught another tear on his fingertips. "I can't be languishing away in an office, number crunching for all eternity. I can feel my soul fragmenting and wasting away. I can't pretend to bang up bad guys, be a superhero whilst filling in spreadsheets. No idea when I'll get on the course at the training college, but I hope to. I want to get onto a course, be a police officer."

Padmi's shoulders fell away from his curled digits. He felt the lowering of her hackles; they had been raised to full mast. Now, her hackles had dropped to resting. His heartrate had settled too, but did nothing to burn away the blur of Padmi having thought the worst.

"I've seen the picture," sniffed Padmi, pressing her lips together and trapping a tear on the tip of her tongue. "The one on Nani's mantelpiece, where you're a little boy holding a Policeman's helmet. You look ready to pace the thin blue line. You really aren't going to dump me. Not today, the day before Valentine's day?"

"Not today," Gorbind whispered, leaning in to kiss her tear-stained lips. "Not ever," he added, pulling Padmi entirely into his arms, almost off her feet. Holding her close, he really didn't want to let her go. He had meant what he had said; there was no dumping. Not now or ever.

"You're my whole world, Padmi," he said softly, something had caught the back of his throat. Gorbind bit the inside of his cheek. "Where ever I go, whatever I do, I'm not doing it without you. I really didn't want to make you cry, I didn't mean to." Pulling back a little, he once more held her by her shoulders. Once more, they were in the middle of swarming, school children.

"They got sharks here, Gorbind?" asked Padmi, her

eyes were bleary and she sobbed in a rather staccato fashion.

Gorbind nodded, rubbing away one last tear. "There's one," he started, "That's slightly crazy, swims around in circles, all day, every day."

Padmi planted a hand onto the curve of his left shoulder. "Do you want to point him out to me," she said with a snort. "I've never seen one up close."

Smiling slightly, he scooped her hand into his.

Psychotic fish he could deal with. A broken Padmi on the other hand, utterly terrified him.

CHAPTER 14

Rinsing off his razor, Gorbind shook off excess water to press the blade against his right cheek. His whole face was lathered with pale green shaving cream. He would have passed for a very badly made up clown.

"What exactly are you doing tonight?" Padmi's voice was a clear as a bell. She could have been right here in the bathroom with him.

Gorbind imagined that she might have been sat upon the toilet behind him; she'd have put the seat down and be talking to him as she applied her makeup. That did actually happen at times, making the imagined tableau that bit more realistic in his head. For the moment, he had only her voice on loud speaker rather than her actual, physical form. His 'phone sat on the cistern whilst propped up against the wall.

"Going to be Arjun's wing-man," he replied, dragging the razor across his skin to sweep a stripe of the black-blue beard that Padmi wrinkled her nose at. There was just something about his facial furniture that mortally offended the woman he loved.

"You having a shave, it's all echo-y," she said, her statement brimming with curiosity. "Good," she added. "You look far prettier without it."

Gorbind dunked his razor into water; shaking it off again, he continued to de-beard himself. "Yep, Arjun doesn't like it either. Said he wanted a pretty wingman; great minds do think alike. He reckons that would improve his chances."

"I get the pretty," Padmi laughed, the sound bouncing across the tiles. "If you are pretty, you might be a little bit more persuasive. Just remember one thing, though."

"Whassat?" asked Gorbind, pulling faces and seeing them in their full contorted glory in the bathroom mirror.

"Arjun might be fishing for his next jock-dropper," replied Padmi, "But you're taken. The only person that you drop your jocks for is me. Okay?"

Gorbind had been about to giggle, but he realised that he had something sharp pressed to his face. He held his resolve for a moment to compose himself.

Gorbind swept the blade a few times to clear the one side of his face.

"Yes, dear," he said finally uttered. "I won't be dropping my jocks for anyone but you, tch," rolling his eyes, he was curious as to where she had got the phrase. It didn't sound particularly classy or pleasant for that matter.

"Good, I'm glad we got that straightened out," Padmi sighed gently across the line. "Dance a bit, won't you. You've not done that for ever. Have a good time, by all means. Whatever you do, no drinking for England. Your liver, like the rest of you, belongs to me."

He made no reply as he concentrated on not slicing his nose off. Dancing was far lower on his list of priorities than drinking was. Dancing with his bother on a night out was never pretty. Generally, being out with Arjun involved copious amounts of alcohol. Sometimes, alcohol was imbibed for courage. Other times, it helped to forget the badly made moves as well as the encounters to close to recall accurately.

"Have you seen my jeans?" Arjun all but took the door off its hinges as he swept in all very dramatically.

"Gorbind winced; a red pearl bloomed at his cheekbone. In the mirror, he saw a half dressed Arjun. His tufty hair had been tweaked into a perfectly formed quiff that swept a little to the left.

"Ironing board," Gorbind and Padmi chorused. He saw Arjun startle in surprise before looking at the 'phone sat on the cistern.

"Cheers," grinned Arjun, slamming the door to exit as quickly as he had arrived.

"Gorbind?" The way Padmi uttered his name mad his spine tingle, the hairs on his arms stood up too. Even the beating of his heart took in a different timbre.

"Yeah?" dabbing a towel to his cheek, Gorbind stemmed blood that was about to trickle down his face.

"Look after him," replied Padmi, worry crackled across the line. "He's a good talker, has the swagger of a champion; but he's easily broken by a bad set of balls. Keep him safe, yes?"

Letting out a deep breath, Gorbind looked at his 'phone on the cistern. She really might as well have been sat there, looking at him whilst applying mascara; Padmi would have pinned him to the spot and not let him go until she had answer in the affirmative.

"Babe, I gotta go," she blew a kiss; he could hear it implode from her lips. "Love you."

As she hung up, Gorbind bit the inside of his cheek. It worried him that Padmi worried. Not everyone had a gay, younger brother, least of all someone of Indian ascent. He understood though, why she worried. He worried for the same reason. They both cared about Arjun, so much that it almost hurt.

CHAPTER 15

"I'm okay, I'm fine," slurred Arjun. His limbs disagreed and weren't under his control as he stumbled down a narrow staircase.

"Then how many fingers am I holding up?" Gorbind had one arm curled around Arjun's waist. With his free arm, he waggled three digits before Arjun's rather flushed face.

"Three?" squinted Arjun, swaying side to side, miss stepping too. "Four perhaps, it's gone very dark and fuzzy."

Slowly but surely, Gorbind helped Arjun down the stairs; the pair of them moved through a crowded room of people dancing. All around them, bodies curved and contorted in plumes of white smoke to the sound of deep based music that thundered along to flashing lights.

"What time is it?" asked Arjun, his weight resting heavily against Gorbind.

"Two, may be three," Gorbind, rolled his eyes but tried to keep calm. "This isn't worth it," he said quietly. "You're completely blotto; I'm getting too old for this nonsense. Plus, plus I am a bit tired of having my backside eyeballed. This is going to flaming well hurt in the morning." Draping his brother's arm around his shoulder, Gorbind picked his way through the heaving bodies to move towards the door.

"I only wanted a laugh," muttered Arjun. His expression was wearied now. Complete inebriation had kicked in as the cold wind hit him the face. "I just wanted to dance around a bit."

Something made Gorbind look around; the hairs on the back of his neck were standing on end. They were stood on the other side of town, surrounded by neon lights that lined narrow side-streets that loomed towards pockets of darkness. It was probably a five, ten minute walk to the nearest taxi rank. All he had to do was walk Arjun there and keep both of them in one piece. Gorbind kept his counsel as they walked. The bright, brash, neon lights of the club district gave way to street lights that seemed to sulk as the stood sentry in the darkness.

The odd car, most likely a taxi, trundled past as they walked in silence. Gorbind could feel alcohol and anxieties collide around his crown; he was concentrating on keeping his eyes and his ears open. Something had him hypervigilant. Something had him on edge and he really didn't like it.

First there were cat-calls. Then there were heavy, thunderous footsteps. After that, kicking and screaming and battered bodies.

Arjun had turned the air blue, thrown a few punches before landing in a crumpled heap.

Gorbind had swung hard a couple of times too; his knuckles were grazed and groaned in being scratched raw.

This had been a full scale fist fight in a murky, maddening darkness.

A car had hooted its horn. Gorbind shielded his eyes as headlights swept across the melee. The full beam illuminated the men, the madness and one hell of a mess.

He heard footsteps again, headed off into the darkness away from him and his brother. No sooner had the bother boots arrived, had they flown off to flee into the night.

Thrown to the floor, Gorbind had landed across Arjun. Together in a heap, they looked at one another. They were both dazed, confused. They pair of them were bruised, battered, brother-in-arms. Pulling Arjun closer, Gorbind wiped blood from his brother's nose.

Arjun's face crumpled, Gorbind bit his lip. He was convinced that his heart had cracked down the middle. Throwing his arms around Arjun, he realised that they were both shaking, both were defeated and going into shock.

Behind them, a taxi parked up with its hazard lights flashing. Blue-eyed soul streamed from the stereo over the snap, crackle and pop of the taxi's radio. A driver exited, thudded his door close to venture towards them.

Arjun sobbed into his shoulder. Gorbind closed his eyes, shushing him gently.

All they had wanted was a nice night out.

CHAPTER 16

Standing over a sink, Gorbind examined his reflection in a rectangular mirror that was riveted to the wall. Passing a thumb across the stitches just above his eyebrow, he was trying very hard not frown and pull anything. The cut had looked far worse than it actually was. His eye was now going a shade of purple best described as being mulberry with a hint of purple.

Behind him to his right, Arjun sat shirtless with his feet dangling over the edge of a hospital bed. His entire torso was dotted with bruises. There were a cluster of angry red marks across his stomach that lined up neatly to form the impression of a boot.

"If that scars, I'll never forgive you."

Gorbind's eyes darted to the left of the mirror. Padmi stood at the curtain. Her face was the same colour scarlet as the smudges of blood that streaked across his pale blue shirt. He watched her come in, pull the curtain closed and head towards Arjun.

"I didn't mean for him to get hurt," Arjun told Padmi; his bottom lip trembled. "He was only looking after me. Padmi, Gorbind always looks after me. He is the only big brother I have. Please don't be pissed at him."

"Sweetie, it's okay," Padmi tutted softly as she swept her arms around Arjun to comfort him. "I know; he loves you very much," she said, smoothing down his ruffled hair. "We both do," Padmi closed her eyes as Arjun's face sank to her shoulder where he sobbed uncontrollably.

Gorbind tried to take in a deep breath, only to wince; there was searing pain across his chest. Placing his left palm to his breastbone, he remembered that he too was bruised and one of his ribs was broken. He watched, listened too. He had called Padmi as soon as they had got to A&E. There, he and Arjun had been looked over and were now ready to go. Padmi was their lift home, not to mention the rescue remedy that Gorbind was quite literally aching for.

"We'll get you home." Padmi said looking at him over her shoulder. "Safe and sound," she added, handing

Arjun his shirt. She inclined her head towards the curtain.

Gorbind took the hint and sloped off out of the cubicle.

Padmi joined him a minute later; he all but fell into her arms. He could barely supressed the pain as she found his broken ribs and held him tightly.

"I tried," Gorbind struggled to breathe through sobs. His face was pressed against Padmi's hair. "I did my best to get him home safely. I did everything I could to smack them sideways, to get away. I really didn't want tonight to end this way, Padmi," he sniffed loudly, wrinkling up his nose. "He's my brother, my flesh and blood. No one gets to treat him this way. So what, if he's gay, he's not hurting anyone."

Once he had finished, Gorbind felt his knees give way. He was half way to the floor before Padmi managed to bundle him into plastic chair by the wall. The next thing he knew, she was in his lap with her palms pressed to his face.

"No one gets to hurt him, Padmi," whispered Gorbind. "I won't let them, I just can't."

He couldn't speak any more, he was shaking again. The trembling was a combination of fear and fury. With no strength to resist, he licked tears from his lips as Padmi wiped away those falling from his eyes. She was close enough to feel his broken heart and the rest of him throb. All he had wanted to do was to look after Arjun. That was all that Padmi had asked of him. He had failed, big time.

CHAPTER 17

Gorbind stomped his green, wellington boots as he pulled up the furry hood of his cagoule. His other hand was not so free either. Padmi swung it back and forth between them. They were trekking through sodden grass and sludgy mud that were something a music festival staple.

"Once in a life time," Padmi had said. "No cushy B&B," she had continued. "Tell Arjun, I'll need his three-man tent. You snore when you are shattered, and I'll need the elbow room so that I don't kick you into the cold."

As with all of Padmi's plans, Gorbind had gone with the flow. As of yet, he had never said no to anything. It was more than his life's worth to ever disagree.

Overhead, clouds loomed. Thunder and lightning had been forecast for the whole weekend.

As he and Padmi trudged, the heavens opened and rain descended. Gorbind could feel the drops lash against his coat. There was also freshness on the wind that gave the rain a little more bite; a bite that stung his cheeks and made him wrinkle up his nose.

They had just left one of the major stages. Both of them were feeling the warming, dis-inhibiting effects of having had several bottles of perry and beer. Gorbind raised his as Padmi stopped dead in her tracks; their hands were mid-swing as thunder cracked in the clouds above. She dropped his hand, to sidle up close. His immediate response was to pull her close. Gorbind counted the seconds to the next rumble. The storm didn't sound too far away.

He didn't have to count very much, there was another crack that distracted his brain entirely. Unzipping a pocket, he pulled out his 'phone with it's battery at thirty-three per cent.

"Tell me you don't want to take pictures?" scoffed Padmi, struggling with her hood.

Ignoring her discord, Gorbind gave a wry smile as he went through his music library.

"Nothing so mundane," he said, his phone was now playing *that* song about making moves in the rain.

"Seriously?" squeaked Padmi.

"Seriously," he replied, dropping his 'phone into his pocket with the music still playing. "Once in lifetime, you said," he held out a hand to take a slight step back to feign chivalry. "When was the last time that you danced in the rain?"

Padmi peered at his hand from beneath her hood.

Raindrops landed with sharpness in his open palm. A pool was starting to form across his heart line.

"If I catch a cold," she said, relenting as she put her palm into his.

"Sue me!" yelled Gorbind, pulling Padmi into hold whilst cobbling together the best bit of footwork that he could. Trudging along in mud, this was not exactly strictly ballroom.

They danced long after the song had ended. Laughing and swaying, they even managed a rendition of 'The Birdy Dance' before bundling in to Arjun's three-man tent. For that moment, they were drunk, wet and a little muddy. None of it mattered.

It would take another day or so before the common cold made its appearance. Music festivals and memories would make the headache and impending bogey that bit worthwhile.

CHAPTER 18

Every inch of him hurt. First, he slid his right leg out from beneath the covers to lower it down onto his bedroom floor. Gorbind had swung his limb out with effort, not to mention a wing and a prayer for it to land where he wanted it. He shuffled his foot a few times; yes, it was definitely on the floor. For two minutes, he willed his body to charge up quickly. Second, he hauled the rest of him up and out of bed, flinging the covers away.

All of that movement caused flames of absolute agony to surge up his arm. This sensation then collided with a leaden heaviness across his chest. His other three limbs felt equally agonised. His chest felt tight, his breathing was laboured. Passing a palm across his face, Gorbind caught a string of mucus streaming from his nose. Bogey had combined with a hot, sticky, sheet of sweat that had formed a film across his skin. His head throbbed; it seemed to hum with fervour as he tried to focus on his bedroom door. Everything hurt so much. Gorbind had no idea if he was able to get to his feet, get to the door.

He might have to crawl. He didn't particularly fancy his chances.

Gorbind felt like death warmed up and ready to crank the boiler. Placing his palms either side of him, he would do his best to haul his mass up towards the door.

Only he heard his 'phone vibrate on his bedside cabinet.

The caller ID told him that it was Padmi's father calling. He vaguely remembered having exchanged numbers, a just-in-case measure. If anything happened, to him, to Padmi, Subash had a way of getting in touch. Seeing Subash's name flash made his stomach pull taut. The way Gorbind felt, his guts were like to lurch up, out and onto carpet anyway.

Gorbind picked up the device, swiped and pressed it to his ear.

"Hello?" he grunted across the line. It hurt to form words and utter them.

"Incoming."

The word meant nothing.

"And you sound awful," said Subash, not pulling any punches. "You sound just as bad as Padmi, actually. She's on her way."

"She's what?" croaked Gorbind, coughing away phlegm.

"Padmi is on her way to you," continued Subash. A brief silence suggested that he was thinking. "She woke up feeling like death warmed up; she looked it too, to be honest with you. I've never seen her in such a mood either. Her mother did try to send her back to bed; but no, she packed a bag, got into her car saying you had to look after her. That this was your entirely fault."

"Uhoh," Gorbind half groaned, rubbing his stubbly cheek. Some part of him should have known this would happen.

"Uhoh indeed," Subash laughed across the line. "All that partying and dancing in the rain that you pair did. Well, Gorbind, your chickens have come home to roost. You've got the best part of ten-fifteen minutes before she gets to you. Good luck there, son."

And with that, Subash hung up.

Gorbind had to first muster up the energy to get to

his feet, then it was a case of making it down the stairs.

Then, then he had to brace for the incoming storm that was Typhoon Padmi.

CHAPTER 19

Slowly but surely, Gorbind got up off his bed.

Somehow, he put his hand to the multi-coloured, crocheted, blanket that was sat on his bed to cloak it around himself. Pulling the blanket tightly around him, he felt heaviness against his shoulder-blades.

As he opened his bedroom door, the hinges creaked; the sound went straight through him. The pitch offended his ears, causing Gorbind to grumble and grimace. Lumbering side to side, Gorbind edged across the landing to make it half way down the stairs.

There he sat, there he lay in wait.

He would stay there until Padmi arrived.

She would most likely be a damp squib too, or at least

he hoped so. He really didn't fancy Padmi the full blown Typhoon. If she had as much bogey, phlegm that he did, they would be equally matched in some sense. They both had the same handicap, perhaps things wouldn't be as tumultuous as Subash had implied.

Subash had given him ten to fifteen minutes as Padmi's estimated time of arrival. If she was feeling half as rough as he was, this might easily extend to twenty minutes; especially as the morning school run was only just starting to subside. Resting a bony elbow onto his knee, Gorbind settled his chin into cupped hand. Training his gaze on the fish-eye in the middle of his door, he watched intently.

He wanted to see her darken his doorstep.

He wanted to hear her rattle his letterbox.

She would probably jab at his doorbell.

Padmi knew exactly how hard to thump his door to get this attention.

Time seemed to slow down, drape itself across his shoulders. The seconds, minutes clung to the lacework of the woollen blanket that cocooned him.

A shadow appeared. He saw it form in the corner of a frosted panel. It soon got bigger, moved and then all four panels within the door went dark.

She was here.

His doorbell screeched a staccato rhythm. A series of three blows rained against the door. The letterbox rattled a vibrato. It's fluttering, metallic, clang drove Gorbind from his position on the stairs. Ignoring the searing pain that danced up his femurs, he bundled down the stairs towards the door.

Clamping his hand around the handle, he fiddled furiously with the mortice lock. Gorbind was frustrated by a fever that quite literally made him all fingers and thumbs; he couldn't open the door quick enough.

When he did open it, the door was flung back with ferocity.

"Ah gotta cold," he said hoarsely, his nose running.

"And me," nodded Padmi. Her nose was red raw, her eyes pink rimmed and looked very sore. She was also drenched. Behind her, the rain was coming down in sheets onto the pavement. Falling in stair rods, it thumped onto the parked cars that lined the street.

Opening up his arms, Gorbind spread out the fabric of the crocheted blanket. For all of two seconds, he felt as though he was playing The Angel Gabriel.

"If it's the same," sniffed Gorbind. "We should probably share it."

It took a supreme effort not to fall over backwards as Padmi bounded into his arms, into the blanket that he swathed around them both.

"Want to look after me?" he asked, his face was pressed into her damp, rain-sodden hair. There was just something comforting about the coldness of the raindrops clinging to her locks.

"Only if you look after me," Padmi croaked. She sounded as bad as him; bogey impeded her articulation to clip clean away the edges of her usually crisp pronunciation.

"I want fish and chips, Gorbind," she snorted and sniffed, her head was pressed into his shoulder.

"Chilli sauce?" he posed. "Hold on. It's raining outside, and neither one of us needs to take walk in this weather. How about left over biryani?" asked Gorbind, absently mindedly fiddling with a lock of her hair. "Nani sent me some. It's meaty, spicy, and full of soul-warming goodness."

"Will it shift our colds?" Padmi wrinkled her nose to look up at him.

"With bells on," he replied with a firm nod. "It works every time."

Padmi untangled herself from his arms, and took his hand in hers. Raindrops fell into his palm as she led them both down hall and into the lounge.

CHAPTER 20

Loosening his garnet-coloured tie, Gorbind kicked his front door closed whilst dropping his keys into a bronze bowl next to it. Something had felt distinctly off today. He had a heavy feeling of unease as he pulled his 'phone from his pocket. His phone had barely rang or vibrated today. For the first time in a long time, Padmi hadn't called or sent a message during the day.

Gorbind double checked his messages, calls, voice messages and even his email.

There was nothing; not a single sausage.

Glancing at the red-framed clock in the hall way, he saw that it was only six p.m. There was usually a message at half five. Sometimes, it would be a half an essay, telling him all about her day. Occasionally, her message might simply be an emoji and he could leave it at that. Walking towards the kitchen, he checked his call registry again.

The last call was at midnight. They'd both hung up at half past. He'd been half asleep when Padmi had called. She had sounded edgy. He knew that he should have registered then that something wasn't right. Gorbind tucked his 'phone back into the pocket of his navy trousers. He opened the 'fridge to take out a bottle of beer. Pulling off the cap, he leant against the sink to take a slug. He thought about the horrible gnarling feeling that was developing just below his kidneys.

Something just wasn't right.

He simply couldn't put his finger on it.

Gorbind was half way down the bottle of beer when his brain began to throb.

What had happened exactly?

Did he say, do something stupid?

Had he forgotten something?

Were they in the middle of a fight that he didn't know about?

Was this one of those stupid tests, where he was

supposed to read Padmi's mind?

Once more, Gorbind pulled out his 'phone. This time he found Padmi on his speed dial. If he didn't try, he would never know.

He was about to press call, only for the sound of a rattling letterbox stop him. His doorbell was also being mercilessly poked at and chimed noisily.

Gorbind wasn't expecting anyone. He pressed call on his 'phone anyway as he opened the door; the device was pressed tightly to his ear. The call rang out. Normally, Padmi might pick up by two rings. After six, he was being asked to leave a message.

As the door swung open, there she was standing on the step. Padmi's eyes had a distinct pink hue to them and matched the flush across her face. Her shoulders were sagging and she clutched a white, plastic, carrier bag flat against her chest.

"Let me in," she said hoarsely. "We need to talk."

CHAPTER 21

Sitting on the edge of the bath, Gorbind had his hands clasped around his left knee. In the middle of the bathroom, his 'phone was sat on a grey bath mat. A timer ha d been set and it was counting down from five minutes. The countdown felt as though the whole of eternity was seeping slowly through the eye of a needle.

Padmi paced from the toilet towards the sink. She had been doing that for the last fifteen minutes.

She had already taken two tests at home. That's what Gorbind had been told in the throes of a high pitched, frenetic melt down where Padmi had nearly wrenched his arms from their sockets. One had been taken last night, just before she called him at midnight. The second was done this morning.

"I don't get it," she said throwing her hands in the air. "How can you just sit there, as calm as anything? You've not twitched, broken sweat, gone as white as sheet. You've not so much as batted an eyelid."

Gorbind half shrugged, his shoulders were awfully stiff and sore after the drama earlier. "You'd said the two you did were negative. We've done one here, that's negative," he waggled a finger at the test sat on the cistern. That one should be too," there was indeed another on the closed down toilet seat. "Technically, we're looking at a lot of negatives. Those tests weren't the cheap false-positive things either. Proper, all singing, all dancing, could almost boil a kettle if they were that intelligent sort of tests. Technically…."

Padmi stopped mid-pace to look at him, all too aghast. "Technically?!" she shrieked. "What do you mean, technically?" she broached him on his bath-edge seat, to loom over him. Now was not the time to tell her how much she looked like a banshee tripping on acid.

"Technically, Gorbind," she said huffing "If it's positive, we have a problem." Stepping away, Padmi scooped her hair from her face as her tone quivered. Her palms the settled at her forehead in sheer desperation.

Uncrossing his legs, Gorbind stood to slide her hands away. He pulled a face, wondering if she had washed them.

"Their clean," tutted Padmi. "I did wash them; that much I do know."

"Good, I'm so glad," he couldn't help but laugh as he sandwiched her hands in his. "If it's positive, it's positive. I don't see the problem."

"You don't?" Padmi recoiled, taking his hands with her. "We'd be having a baby, a little human being. We'd being having a child out of wedlock, Gorbind. I don't know which bit is worse; which bit will make people talk the most."

This time, Gorbind shrugged properly.

"Let them," he declared. "This wouldn't be the first baby to be born out wedlock, sure as hell won't be the last. Might cause a bit of drama, a bit of Bollywood drama, but so what? That's the best kind of drama. The sort of drama makes the world a little bit more interesting. No one likes vanilla, not really."

Padmi nailed him once more with a look of sheer horror. "I don't get it," she said rubbing her eyes. "I've been stressing all day, trying not to think of the potential Bollywood drama, and here you are, just naming it."

Gorbind's 'phone vibrated on the mat. The device was hoping around a bit too excitedly for Gorbind's liking.

Both of them ran to the toilet seat.

He scooped the test up into his hands. Padmi leant against him, her head buried into the space between his shoulder blades. She had grasped a wad of his shirt and managed to grab some skin as well. One day, he would show Padmi the scratches. The woman really didn't know her own strength.

Raising a brow, Gorbind peered at the LCD panel.

"Tell me," Padmi queried, her words were somewhat muffled. "If you so much as think about taking the micky; so help me God, I will hurt you, Gorbind Phalla."

The thought had actually crossed his mind. Some part of him wanted to draw this out to increase the dramatic tension.

"It's," he took in a deep breath.

Padmi pinched the top of his right hip and held the flesh hard between her fingertips.

"Negative," declared Gorbind, unable to bear the searing pain. "We're not having a little human. Not yet anyway. Jesus, all that drama." Reaching onto the toilet cistern, he plucked up the other test to lob both into the pedal bin by the sink.

He almost fell over Padmi who had sunk to her knees. That was enough to scare him witless as Gorbind scooped her up into his arms and out of the bathroom. Moving quickly, he all but threw her onto his bed.

That was probably what caused all of this in the first place.

Gorbind wasn't about to mention that as he vaulted onto the bed alongside her. Padmi was shaking; all he could do was hold her.

"Can we do this again later, bur properly?" she asked, half sobbing, half stuttering. "I really don't want all that stupid Bollywood drama, Gorbind, do you know what I mean? That would break me."

"No drama," whispered Gorbind, absent mindedly running his fingers through the ends of her hair. "We can do this much later, yes. You can tell me then, what you mean by properly, but yes. Whatever you say, sweetheart. Not a problem."

"Properly means wedlock, Gorbind," Padmi nudged his knee sharply with her toe.

"I know," he let out a sigh as she nudged her hip. "Still not a problem, and all in good time. I take it you want babies. We've never actually had that particular conversation. Well, not at length and as a three-dimensional reality. "

"And not having conversation," Padmi spoke as she shifted a little on her side. "That's what started this whole little episode in the first place. Yes; yes, I do want babies. Do you?" she asked, sitting up against cushions to look down at him.

Slouching backwards, he had seen her hand heard towards a pillow. The wrong answer would mean assault with a not so deadly weapon. She had managed to grab a corner.

"Yes," he replied, "But I don't particularly want to father a whole football team. Please don't ask me how many. Whatever we get, we get. I've got you, everything else, anything else, would be a bonus."

Gorbind saw Padmi's grip on the pillow relax; she let go and shuffled back into his arms.

"Good answer," she said quietly. "Babies, will definitely be a bonus."

CHAPTER 22

"GORBIND, STOP! Watch what you're doing!" Padmi yelled.

Her tone was harsh, abrupt enough to wake him from a very frenzied sleep.

Gorbind snapped his eyes open to wake. He tried to sit up properly; only Padmi was bearing down on him heavily. Her hands were curled around his wrists. His arms were stretched out towards hers; the rest of him was splayed beneath the covers. Gorbind really couldn't move. Banked up behind him was a mountain of pillows. He hated the pillows, but put up with them as this wasn't his room.

He and Padmi were in Nani's second bedroom. Gorbind was in no position to argue about the fluffy stack. They had both stayed over as tomorrow was something of an important day. His brother was asleep next door in the spare room.

This was however, the first time that Padmi was staying here. He had been rather surprised that Nani had invited Padmi to stay. Gorbind had been even more surprised that Nani hadn't launched him towards the sofa. There had been no quoting of archaic norms and values. Since Nani had taken Arjun coming out in her stride, there were clearly no bones to be made. There was no mention of wedding bells being the mandatory requirement for him and Padmi sharing her second bedroom.

Looking altogether dishevelled, Padmi stared at him all wide-eyed. Her dark locks were tempestuously untamed about her face; a few strands had fallen across her eyes. Letting go of his wrists, she thrust his limbs back at him. Pulling a face, she then used her hands to push her hair aside.

"What's the matter with you?" she hissed, pulling the light-weight duvet that Gorbind had churned up in his sleep. "Tossing, turning; you've kicked at me like a mule. And you've tried to shove me out too," Padmi frowned as she sharply jabbed a toe into his knee. "You're not always like this, hopping around like a toad on acid," she said huffing heavily.

Hair fell across her face again. Padmi scooped it all backwards with her palm. Tugging the duvet tighter she covered her shoulders. With a manicured finger, she slid up the straps of her midnight blue night dress. She shuffled closer towards Gorbind beneath the covers. Padmi looked wary, but wrapped his one arm around her anyway.

With his free hand, Gorbind used the heel of his palm to rub his eye. "Night terror," he replied, yawning. "Haven't had one in years. You didn't break anything, did you?" Gorbind blinked once again, this time to focus on Padmi's bleary eyes. "When I was eleven, I bounced out of bed and broke my arm. It wasn't pretty."

Padmi dramatically raised the duvet to take a look below. "Don't think I'll bruise," she said looking back up at him. "I'd ask if you want restraining; only you might enjoy it."

"Well," Gorbind raised a brow as much as he could. "I've read the trilogy. I don't fancy the chaffing. That really wouldn't help," he said shaking his head. "Childhood trauma due to parental death is probably not best dealt with by a bit of S&M."

Padmi blew air across her teeth. "Is that what it is? I'm sorry, I didn't realise, Gorbind."

He caught her rolling her eyes; that was probably her kicking herself.

"You've never said before," she continued, rather

cautiously. "You don't really talk 'bout...."

"Mugging gone wrong," Gorbind interjected; it was now or never. The woman he loved, had every right to know why he had kicked out in his sleep. His hand had somehow ended flat on Padmi's stomach, where she was fiddling with his fingers. "We'd been here eight months, and Mum was walking on the canal tow path on her way back home from the factory. A stoner crossed her path, pulled out a knife. Apparently, Mum resisted; she wasn't going to hand her jewellery over without a fight. There was a struggle, she got hurt. Nani gave her that jewellery. Dad couldn't take it when he was drunk, gambling away the mortgage. There was no way that some jack-ass reprobate would get it."

It all came tumbling out; this was what he had kept from her for all this time. He had held onto it, held it tightly against his chest in something of a protective measure. Some part of him was relieved to finally let go, to finally show Padmi some of his rather significant cards.

"I never sleep properly the night before," he said softly. "Never have done."

There was more. This all needed to come out. Padmi needed to know everything.

"She didn't come home," Gorbind spoke over a long,

out-going breath. "Nani was really worried. She paced up and down, wringing her hands for ages. I remember that so vividly," he couldn't help but nod as his brow furrowed. "Then there was the 'phone call. I heard the God-awful shriek and I ran down the stairs. Nani was at the bottom, she'd dropped it. She'd dropped the 'phone on the floor and was sobbing her heart out. It was the police."

Gorbind stopped, stopped to draw breath; his chest rose high before falling to his stomach. "I picked it up, said hello to this man on the other end. A copper was talking to me, a bit confused as to where Nani went. It took him a moment to realise that I was a kid. I explained how Nani didn't always understand English." Gnarling at his lip, he steadied himself, gulping away phlegm that formed in his throat. "I told him, that she knew bits and pieces. He took some details. Half an hour later, he and a family liaison officer were here. Nani called my Leela Massi and that was it. From that point onwards, everything went completely and utterly pear-shaped."

Slumping backwards, he closed his eyes as Padmi put her hand to his chest. Her hand was directly over his hard-beating heart. Everything was now all out in the open.

"Thing is, Padmi," he said quietly, "When you're a kid, no one tells you anything. No one expects you to understand; so there's no point in saying anything.

Nani shut up shop immediately. Her daughter was dead; murdered. "Leela Massi...." Padmi had slid closer and closer around him, her hand travelled to his sternum.

"I remember Massi hugging me so hard that I thought one of us might break," continued Gorbind. "She told us that Mummy had gone to heaven because of a very bad man. I was sixteen before she told me the full story. She had to at that point," he puffed out his cheeks to blow out air. "The chap in question was about to be released."

Gorbind heard his heart race; he could feel it throb painfully. He was convinced that each heart beat tightened his ever stretched heart-strings. Heart-strings that had been pulled so taut over the years, he figured that one day they might snap when he least expected it.

"She came here, armed with a bottle of Jack Daniels," Gorbind half laughed. "Sat me down in the kitchen, poured me some fizzy pop and dosed it with two fingers of hooch. It was a Friday night, so there was no danger of me wagging school the next day whilst under the influence. Leela gave me the whole sorry saga from start to finish." He scooped away tears from the hollows of his eyes; two of which flew from his fingers to be absorbed into the duvet.

"She told what happened on the day mum died, how

she-Leela Massi- then fought with Nani about Arjun and I going to the funeral. Nani refused point blank," he sobbed freely now, his voice breaking. "Arjun and I were sent to the Nature centre and then the Museum in town after. Not even to school, but somewhere safe. Somewhere sadness, murder and misery couldn't touch us. To this day, Massi is fuming that we didn't get to properly say our goodbyes. As a grown up," Gorbind gulped, licking away tears from his lip. "As grown up, I do actually get it."

"That explains the museum," Padmi finally offered. "That makes complete sense now. She really bought you booze?" He heard the delicate flutter of her eyelashes as she asked.

"Yep," nodded Gorbind. "She's the only aunt I know who takes a stash to weddings. She conceals it in her clutch, makes sure that there's always a bottle of cola around to disguise it. My Aunty Leela is the ultimate rebellious Bollywood Aunty. That day, in the kitchen she became a hero and I will always appreciate it."

"Tomorrow, my sweet, is Mum's anniversary," he said putting a hand to Padmi's on his chest. "Every year, I tell myself that it will get easier. That somehow, some of the pain will go. It doesn't, it hasn't," Gorbind shook his head slowly. "Every year, we go to the Gurdwara, we listen, have langhar. Take Nani out for tea and samosas in the evening. We might even go to the memorial garden before tea time, if Nani feels up to it. Dad turns up too, from time to time."

Padmi looked up, her head tilted backwards. "He does, doesn't he," there was a distinct agitated tone to her voice as she spoke.

"He does," nodded Gorbind. "Usually he is as drunk as a skunk. He'll rock up here, shouting all sorts under the sun. Once or twice, Arjun has threatened to lay him out cold. Either I've had to peel him off or Nani has called the police. You saw him last year; you saw first-hand what happens.

Padmi settled back down into his arms, once more fiddling with his fingers.

"One of these days, Padmi," Gorbind nudged her hip slightly as it poked into his waist. "Arjun will lamp him proper, and I won't get in his way. I won't be able to stop Arjun doing proper damage. I wouldn't stop anyone to be honest, never mind my baby brother. It's Nani that I worry about. For over twenty years, she lived with his drama. She has lived with him sullying my Mum's memory. Every time he shows up, I never know how she's going to handle it. It might be easier for us all, if he was to end up dead in a ditch somewhere." He could feel himself start to vibrate with anger.

"Ssh," Padmi slid up from having been coiled around his trunk. Placing a warm finger to his lips, she shook her head.

"Not a day goes by," continued Gorbind, "When I don't think about her. How Mum might have been with you, with Arjun. I would love to know, what might have been. What Mum would have done in raising us. I miss her, Padmi. I miss my mum." His words ebbed away as his voice crackled and he choked.

Before he knew it, he couldn't hold the torrent back any more. His choking gave way to deep throaty sobs. Once more, Padmi engulfed him in her embrace.

Gorbind was letting go of everything.

If Padmi couldn't catch it all, then no one could.

If she could hold this, all of the hurt that he held inside, then she could hold his whole world. This was a big job, and he couldn't think of anyone better to do it.

As he fell into her arms and a patchy, unsettled sleep, Gorbind actually felt a little lighter. Tomorrow, however, would be a challenge. Sharing had helped. Sleep, even it if were broken would also be useful.

CHAPTER 23

Leaning against the kitchen work top, Gorbind's shoulders slackened to his sides. He nursed a cup of well brewed Chai. Today had been exhausting, least of all due to having nightmares. This particular day and Mother's Day always left him feeling exhausted and beleaguered. Gorbind took a long slurp of hot, spiced tea. Black Cardamom had a hefty clout that was somewhat tempered with fennel and brown sugar. He savoured the soul-soothing flavour, taking solace in the warmth that travelled down his throat.

Sweet, spiced, freshly brewed Chai was Nani's answer to everything.

"Have another," Said Padmi, pressing a balled-up tea-towel onto a chappati. It was rising as it filled with hot air to cook through on a heavy skillet. Sat next to it was a saucepan of almost ochre-coloured liquid that was Chai. A thick, gloopy meniscus had formed across the surface; it dimpled and wrinkled against the side of the pan. "You've barely eaten anything, drank anything; you had next to nothing at the Gurdwara." She had broken Nani's rules, elbowed him out the way and made them all a late lunch.

Gorbind shuffled towards the stove. Plonking a tea strainer onto the mug, he lifted the pan to pour a fresh mugful. As the mug filled, he couldn't help but inhale the heavenly scent that stirred his soul to near Nirvana.

Lifting a cooked chappati between pinching fingers, Padmi dropped it into a blue and white, checked tea-towel resting on a side plate. Positioned nearby was a bowl of yellow lentils. Yellow Dhal was the other answer to everything; it had healing powers when you felt as though you'd been sucker punched in the gut. That was exactly how Gorbind felt today.

"I'll take this in for you, bring your tea," she said putting a hand delicately to his shoulder. "You really need to eat, Gorbind. Tell Arjun too, Nani said she'll eat later."

"Yeah, I will," Gorbind nodded, before turning his head to shout. "ARJUN-"

He was barely able to finish. The sound of the front

door being thumped and thwacked punctured the air to cut Gorbind off.

"Open this door, Gorbind! So help me God"

Kicking and punching continued; the letterbox rattled on its hinges.

"Balls," muttered Gorbind, landing his mug onto the worktop with a thud. "NOT TODAY, GO TO HELL!" he roared. Leaving the kitchen, he stomped and swaggered down the hall to throw open the front door.

"Go home, old man, you're drunk," Gorbind growled and bore his teeth. He had grasped the visitor by the collar to have him on precariouslu balanced on his heels. He thrust the man forward against the passenger side of a blue Ford.

"You do this every year," Gorbind pronounced through gritted teeth. "When will you learn, eh?" Gorbind glared at his drunken, disordered father. He could smell alcohol intermingled with bad breath and stale cigarette smoke.

"You weren't welcome here when Mum was alive," hissed Gorbind, "You'll never be welcome here when she's dead either. What do you want this time?" He hurled the man away from the car and to the pavement. His father was a crumpled mess upon the floor. Gorbind was surprised as to how easily the older man had landed. They were of a similar height, weight too. For once, Gorbind had not realised his own strength.

Arjun thundered out of the front door to stand next to Gorbind. The sleeves of his grey, hooded top were rolled up in anticipation. Things had the potential to become heavy.

"You," sneered the sixty year old man. He looked Arjun up and down with disdain. "You're an abomination," he screamed the words; throwing them against bodies and brickwork. Clambering to all fours, he rose to his feet. Lurching forwards, his fist was curled and headed towards Arjun's face. "You're a disgrace, your kind should-"

Shifting his feet, Gorbind was spurred into action. He wasn't going to stand by when his brother was under attack. Grabbing the fist that was never going to land, he turned his father's arm behind his behind his back to stack him against a brick wall. Baring down, Gorbind heard his father grunt, growl and finally stop resisting.

Gorbind wrenched his father's arm tighter under beneath his shoulder blade. He felt Arjun loom across him. Taking the hint, Gorbind let go a little. He knew that Arjun had something to say, whilst looking their father in the eye.

Flipping the man onto his front, Gorbind choked down hot venom.

"You're the disgrace, Dad," Arjun sounded loudly. "You're the abomination, not me. No self-respecting man beats his wife, scares the crap out of his kids and gets away with it. I'd sooner smack him sideways myself," he said stepping forward, tapping away Gorbind's hand.

He was wary, but Gorbind let go of his father. Standing shoulder to shoulder with Arjun, he saw his brother roll his sleeves up further.

Gorbind arched a brow as Arjun pinned their father back into place against the wall by the shoulders. Arjun's other hand was balled into a fist and pulled back like an arrow at the curve of a bow.

"Go on," sneered the drunk. "Take the shot, Arjun. Hit me, you know you want to." A provocative laugh crackled in the dense air that hung between three men. "Show me how a real man behaves. You're not a real man though, are you? Not really. You're no better than me, you never will be."

"Don't," Gorbind had heard enough, he hauled Arjun back to heel. "He's not worth it, he never will be. We can't do this; not for mum, not today."

Drawing down his fist, Arjun shook his head.

Gorbind leant forward a little, elbowing Arjun out of the way a little. He was once more toe-to-toe with his father. From the corner of his eye, he could see Padmi and Nani standing at the door step watching this whole sorry spectacle.

"Every year, you come back," said Gorbind, rubbing his palms together. "You make a mockery of Mum's anniversary; you remind us of why she left you in the first place. Remind us," he continued, edging closer still to jab a finger into a puffed out chest, "That Arjun and I don't need you. We will never need you. This is the last time I get between you and Arjun, do you understand?" he asked, glaring at deep, chocolate eyes that he had inherited.

"If you come back again, I won't stop him. I'll actually help him. I'll make sure that together, Arjun and I turn you into the same bloody mess that you used to make of Mum. Walk away, Arvind," Gorbind snarled his words. "Get the hell out of here, or so help me God, we send you there in a body bag."

Pulling his father away from the wall, Arvind was hauled onto the pavement.

Arvind staggered to his feet. "You two always were little girls, hiding behind your mother," he slurred, his face contorting it an indignant grimace. "She was as simpering dolt; you two aren't much better."

Gorbind couldn't move quickly enough.

Arjun had bolted. He had landed a heavy upper cut that sent their father sideways into a door.

Clambering after Arjun, Gorbind pulled him back with every sinew pulled taut. Arvind had almost been knocked to the ground, but used the door to pull himself up right.

Gorbind could feel Arjun fume and vibrate in his arms.

"Move whilst you can still walk," Arjun barked. "I'm a bigger, better man than you ever will be. Sod off."

Arvind passed a palm across his bloody nose. He chuntered something that Gorbind couldn't make out, spat at their feet and staggered off down the street.

Gorbind kept a firm hold of Arjun, anchoring him close as their father disappeared around a corner. Arjun wobbled. Gorbind moved swiftly and caught him to catch him just as Arjun's knees gave way entirely.

"He's gone," Gorbind uttered quietly. "It's okay. I got you Arjun, I always got you," wrapping his arms around his baby brother, he could only hold him. Gorbinds let Arjun sob into his arms, not having the heart to shush him.

Punam Farmah

CHAPTER 24

"He is a horrible, horrible man," Nani declared. "No idea why he does this. He has all the sense of a rabid monkey," she continued. Her face was thundery as she wrung the end of her scarf as it lay in her lap.

Gorbind put a mug of hot tea down before her. He arched a brow as his grandmother proceeded to verbally abuse his father using parts of the Punjabi vernacular that made him wince. There were some phrases that he was au fait with, others he thought were wonderfully apt and described his father to a tee. Gorbind squinted at the bits that his brain couldn't quite translate.

"Just sit down," Padmi shoved Arjun into the chair next to Nani at the dining table. "You're shaking," she told him, holding his shoulders to wedge him into the seat. "First aid kit?" she asked, looking directly at Gorbind.

"Kitchen, I'll get it," he said, turning on his heel to go find it. Pulling open the cupboard beneath the sink, he found the battered, Danish butter cookie tin that passed for the first aid kit. The lid was warped and even had a dent where Nani had once hit with a rolling pin. As he returned to the dining table, he couldn't for the life of him remember why the tin had suffered such an indignity.

He prized the lid off with a soft ping. Padmi swooped in to scoop the tin from his hands. Gorbind was left clutching the lid. He was taken aback when the box landed with a thud before his brother.

"You smacked him," said Padmi as she rifled through the tin. "You did yourself some damage; was he really worth it, I mean really, Arjun?" Padmi asked. She had found an alcohol wipe and tore it open. "This is going to sting, young man."

Gorbind watched, all too intrigued as Padmi dabbed at Arjun's grazed hand. His brother winced and pouted as his wounds were tended to.

"That the least of what he deserves," Arjun huffed. He looked very much like a belligerent child being chastised for bad behaviour.

"Agreed," said Gorbind, before turning to

grandmother. "Want whiskey in your tea, Nanu? Where is it exactly?" he asked, putting down the lid of the biscuit tin.

"What, no!" screeched Nani, looking at him aghast. "If you want it, you have it. It's where it is normally. It's somewhere behind all the pots and pans. You'll find it where your Leela Massi hid it. Thinks I don't know, but I do."

Gorbind smirked at the mention of his aunt's name. Stashing the alcohol behind pots and pans was exactly the sort of thing that his mum's sister would do, if only to antagonise his teetotal grandmother. He departed again and rummaged through pans. There he found the three-quarters full bottle of premium grade Scotch. Picking up two tumblers from the drainer, he scooted back to the dining table. Tucking in his lips, he avoided Nani's glare as the glasses was put near the first aid tin.

"I'll have some of yours," Padmi didn't even look at him as she continued to wipe down Arjun's knuckles. "Don't be so daft as to drink it neat."

"Yes, dear," he uttered, retreating to the kitchen for a third time. This time he found a hi-ball glass and filled it with freshly drawn, cold water.

"Nasty stuff, don't see why you people drink it," Nani pulled faces as he arrived back. This was at complete odds with the fact that she had taken the bottle from him to unscrew the cap.

The next thing he saw, she was sloshing some of the contents into glasses.

Padmi was agog as she looked at him. He could only roll his shoulders in a shrug.

"Will rot your insides," commented Nani, "Never mind your soul," she added, putting the bottle down with a clink against the biscuit tin.

Pouring water into the whiskey, Gorbind shook his head at how much Nani had out into the glasses. He nudged one glass towards Arjun to take a slug from his own. Once the glass had left his lips, Padmi leant across to relive him of it.

"Not bad stuff," she said smacking her lips together in appreciation. Handing it back, Padmi smiled. "I always did like your Aunty Leela," she passed the tip of her her tongue across her tongue. It happened all too quickly, but was wonderfully tantalising. It was the thrust of the glass, the coolness of it against his skin that brought him back into the room.

Gorbind plonked himself into a chair next to Nani. She caught him off guard as she clicked her tea against his glass of scotch. Both of them watched as Padmi fussed over Arjun as he continued to pout.

Kangana

CHAPTER 25

By the time dusk fell, the dramatic edge to the day had subsided. Gorbind was nursed yet another cup of tea whilst sat in the garden. A gaggle of geese flew across the orange-pink sky. The colour was very similar to that of the burning flames in the Chiminea on Nani's patio.

His head hummed, his heart hurt. Slurping his tea, Gorbind sat hunched forward in a garden chair.

"Hey," Padmi's hand swept delicately passed his shoulder; it was then pressed between his shoulder blades. She kissed his ear before sitting in the chair next to him. "Arjun has gone to bed; he did down half a bottle of red. Nani has had her dinner, she has also retired. She gave Arjun a long, windy, talking to about the dangers of alcohol. The best bit was her suggestion to land another punch the next time your dad turns up, to make it quicker and harder."

"He will as well," nodded Gorbind as he sat a little more upright. "Dad will definitely turn up again. You saw him last year, drunk and delirious. You saw him today, just as bad. Arjun's been wanting to clock him one for years; I've always managed to stop it from happening. Today, I just wasn't quick enough."

"Doesn't matter," Padmi placed her hand upon his wrist. "Arjun did what he had to; just like you've been doing all these years. You've kept him safe, helped Nani raise him. He's a lot stronger than you give him credit for, Gorbind. To be perfectly honest, you both are."

He watched Padmi draw circles across his forearm. There was something wonderfully soothing about her touch, her words and having her close.

"If and when your Dad turns up," continued Padmi, "We'll deal with him; we'll do it together. All of us, together; because we're family. We battle such crap and nonsense side by side. Side by side, we're stronger. Side by side, we can do anything. Isn't that what Nani says to you, what your mum used to say to you?"

Hearing Padmi say the mantra, he felt something ping inside. His face crumpled, his mouth turned downwards at the corners. Gorbind couldn't hold things back any longer. Hot, salty tears coursed from his eyes; his breath was soaked in spluttering sobs. Padmi's arms engulfed him just as his heart burst. The hurt throbbed in his chest; it throbbed with never having got over the loss of his mother. He had to share it, share it with Padmi and hope that she would help him heal.

CHAPTER 26

Two mugs landed with a clink onto the worktop. Gorbind winced at the sharp, hemisphere-splitting sound. He was more than a little hungover. It took a supreme effort to put one foot before the other. Gingerly, Gorbind tip-toed around his kitchen as he tried to make two, very strong, cups of tea. Every step that he took, unsettled his stomach. As he moved, he silently gulped down the rising contents of a churning gut.

"Davey and Corrine looked sooooo happy," trilled Padmi as she appeared at the kitchen door.

"Hmm," nodded Gorbind, his eyes closed. She was rather loud. Even nodding hurt; it felt as though a giant ball-bearing was sliding around against the walls of his skull. "Tea?" he asked, taking in the sight of a very bedraggled looking Padmi.

She'd stepped into his kitchen wearing his pyjamas under his royal blue, towelling dressing gown. Padmi's dark locks were scrapped back into a pony til, her eyes were ringed with stubborn eyeliner and mascara from the night before.

They had rolled in at three. Her war paint-her words, not his-lingered, all very smudged. They had both been very drunk before going to bed. She had bundled him under the covers. Padmi had then driven them back to his, unable to face breakfast at the hotel.

"I'll do it," she nudged him out the way, directing him toward the sink. "How you are still standing this morning, I don't know. Do you remember doing the time warp at one in the morning?"

Cautiously, Gorbind slowly shook his head whilst leaning against the sink. He didn't want to tip that ball bearing.

He was yet to say anything. He hadn't wanted to go, to the wedding, to the outer limits of the next county. Davey was great, part of his and Padmi's inner circle since university. Corrine too; she'd bee Padmi's wing-woman since they'd first met. It wasn't the bride or groom that bothered him.

It was the whole marriage thing that bothered him. The prospect of marriage had worried him six weeks ago when the ivory and silver invite had been pressed into his palm by Davey. He'd been unsettled by the proposal that had happened in Prague a year ago. Nuptial bliss perturbed him now as he tried to work out how he felt about it all.

Padmi and Corrine had cooed, cackled closely in the run up. Padmi had been privy to almost everything. Everything was subsequently passed on to him. He'd been sworn to secrecy. He was to tell Davey nothing or Padmi would sleep on the sofa indefinitely.

"Leave my tea bag in, please," he uttered hoarsely. "And don't spare the sugar."

Glancing at him over her shoulder, Padmi heaped two tablespoons of sugar into hot, black tea.

He was thankful for tablespoons. She knew his hangovers well. He didn't experience them often, but when he did, Gorbind needed all the help he could get.

Gorbind yawned as he rubbed his eyes with the heels of his palms. "I'm glad it's all over," he said slowly. Letting go of a hot breath, he passed the tip of his tongue across dry, chapped lips. "The run up, the drama," Gorbind stretched his eyes open. "The madness of Corinne having cold feet and Davey panicking when trying to convince her. How they finally managed to say I do, flip only knows. Pure drama, just sends me into a tail-spin just thinking about it. I mean, is it worth it?"

The cat was out of the bag.

Padmi handed him his tea as he threw her something of a pained look.

This however, was going to hurt more than his hangover.

"Isn't that what you want?" asked Padmi, moving strands of hair that had fallen across her eyes. "To get married, celebrate a new beginning with the woman you love. Make a commitment and mean it?"

Gorbind pressed the rim against his lips and lowered his eyes into mug. The heat of the liquid radiated to cut across the sting of chapped skin. His hangover collided with the chaos that came with watching, listening and trying to understand Padmi during the wedding preparations.

"I'm just, just not sure," he whispered, letting tea slip slowly down this throat. He was steeling himself to look at her, be eye to eye with her; only his courage wasn't quite screwed to the sticking place.

Slowly, Gorbind flicked his eyes up.

He saw Padmi step back warily as she picked up her tea.

"Not sure?" she asked, her eyelashes were fluttered in a flurry. "Well, what exactly are we doing Gorbind?" her tone had ratcheted up a notch. "You're meant to be the certain one; the one who knows what he wants and when. So straight-laced, that there was only place that this was ever going to go. Isn't that right? We're meant to go straight down the aisle; with everything being done, quite literally by the book."

Gorbind saw Padmi's knuckles blanch as her grip around the mug of tea intensified.

"That is what I wanted, yes," he replied.

"Wanted, *past tense*?" Padmi shifted forward across the kitchen tiles. "And you don't anymore?" You need to tell me," she said, her chest rising and falling as she drew breath in rapidly. "Has this all been a waste? Did we waste the years that we've spent together, the dates, the weekends. All of the family Diwalis, the Christmas dinners and summer get-togethers were just something and nothing. Did you lead me on into some dream?" The stream of questions trembled from her lips: lips that quivered with the gloss of hot tea.

Padmi's eyes were starting to glisten. He could see a tear bloom, and travel down her nose.

"Straight-laced," Gorbind felt the words grate up his throat before he spat them out.

He'd been called a lot of things before, but never straight-laced. Was he really that mundane, that boring? There was something about being called straight-laced that actually stung.

So much for it being a good thing.

So much for Mr.Nice guy.

"Simple, straight forwards and traditional, Padmi, that's me," he continued. His shoulders tensed, his biceps pinged as he moved away from the sink. "I don't do, don't need drama, frou-frou frivolity that doesn't mean anything. You make me sound….like a box-ticker. I'm not someone who just goes through the motions on auto-pilot."

Pulling his shoulders up and back, Gorbind was still holding onto his tea as though it was a makeshift shield.

"I'm not bland, boring, no frills and all frontal-lobed," his tone rose and thudded across the walls. "Don't settle then, don't settle and for me, Padmi," Gorbind's throat caught slightly as his nostrils flared. "That's really not fair. I guess, I guess that this really has been a waste. I'm sorry." A gurgle from his gut signalled that it was flipping wildly. His throat tightened with each syllable. In his chest, his heart hammered in relief. Everything that he had been thinking, feeling; it was all out.

Gorbind couldn't take it all back, even if he wanted to.

Chewing his lip, he looked into his mug. A soggy tea bag at the bottom didn't look all that pretty. He couldn't bring himself to look at her. To look Padmi in the eye, would have been a step too far. All he heard was Padmi's bare feet shuffling away. She had stepped out of her slippers. Slippers that he had given as a gift last Christmas; they were fluffy, yellow and black, goggle-eyed bumble bees.

She had stepped out of the slippers, his kitchen; within half an hour, Padmi had stepped out of his house.

Padmi had gone and every inch of him hurt. Gorbind howled into the sink. Boring and broken hearted, straight-laced was never going to cut it.

CHAPTER 27

Absent-mindedly, Gorbind flicked between T.V. channels. Curled up in the corner of Nani's sofa, he had a black and blue, stripped blanket draped across his knees. He had called work to fake a sick day before walking here. This was the one place in the whole world that felt like home. This was the one place where Gorbind felt protected; the one place where no one could hurt him. No-one, could hurt him more than he had already hurt himself. More than he had hurt Padmi.

A dysfunctional family appeared on screen and volleyed abuse at one other. As their fight started to build towards a rather ugly crescendo, Nani came in to her living room. In her hands, she held a silver-coloured tray laden with two cups of spiced tea-the signature scent wafted towards him-a plate of jam-filled biscuits as well as a stack of cheese and tomato sandwiches.

This was Nani's ill child survival kit. He hadn't seen that in years. The tray only came out in the most extreme cases. Hangovers didn't count. As far as Nani was concerned, having a hangover was very much self-inflicted. Therefore, the tray was far too special to be wasted upon something so stupid; something that could be very easily avoided.

"Here, you should drink some tea," remarked Nani, putting the tray down onto a coffee table with something of a clang. She picked up a robust looking red mug and handed it over with both of her hands.

Mint. As Gorbind took the mug into his hands, the fragrance hit his nose immediately. Mint tea was Nani's cure for all things gut-sickening. He smiled weakly as heat radiated towards his fingers. He felt gut sick; he probably looked it too.

He was bringing his tea to his lips when Nani put her hand to his forehead. Gorbind almost flinched as she did. In a flash, he was eight years old again.

"You're not hot," Nani commented, frowning as she double checked his temperature. Her hand moved momentarily across his cheek and onto stubble. He'd forgotten to shave; it had seemed a bridge too far when trying to get it here without keeling over.

"A bit cold really," she added, tutting to tilt her head to one side. "I know that you're not hungover; you'd never come here in that state. There's been no vomiting, you've barely moved since you got here. Are you going to tell me what the real problem is, Gorbind?"

He could feel his bottom lip start to tremble. Gorbind's immediate instinct was to try and make it stop. Biting his lip, he put his tea down and shuffled towards Nani. Taking in a deep breath, he could nothing to stop his heart from throbbing; his stomach flipped. He heard the bangles at Nani's wrist jangle as she slid her hands over his. The warmth from the mug of tea was quickly transposed by the warmth of maternal love.

"Nani, I broke it off with Padmi," each word was like a thorn passing between his lips. His words that came out half-strangled, were punctuated by slices of silences and sobs. "I shouldn't have: she's the one, and I'm incredibly stupid. This hurts, Nani, and I don't know what to do. Help me, I feel as though I'm dying."

Nani said nothing as she threw her arms around him.

Gorbind's head fell onto her shoulder. There he sobbed and felt the dark blue depths of self-inflicted heartbreak.

"You are stupid, yes," Nani said quietly, her fingers softly stroked his hair. "You feel as though you're dying. As though you've lost a piece of yourself. Padmi is a part of you. What is it that people say? Your other half. Is that right?"

Gorbind nodded silently, wiping away tears with the back of his hand.

"When you're only half the man you could be, this is what it feels like." Nani sat back a little. Rummaging in the pockets of her Lavender coloured cardigan, she had found a neatly folded up piece of kitchen roll. It had corners that could probably cut through cheese; she held it directly below his nose.

He gulped down bogey to take the tissue. Gorbind looked at Nani through tears that stubbornly clung to his lashes before dabbing at his eyes.

"Make this right," Nani glared at him whilst wagging her finger. "Don't sit here and sulk, young man. You and Padmi belong together, you know that. When the pair of you are together, you laugh, you smile; you look as though Padmi has given you the moon and stars. Don't think I haven't noticed," still her finger wagged with ferocity. "She makes me happy too. When she comes here, the whole house lights up and it feels as though there is a daughter here again. She's a Goddess sent to make this house a home, that's what I believe, Gorbind. And don't get me started on Arjun."

Gorbind grimaced as he tried to breathe. He had not capacity to argue.

"Arjun dotes on her," Nani's cheeks pulled back as she beamed. "Padmi dotes on him. He's finally got a big sister and his world is complete. With Padmi, you are complete. Padmi, makes this family complete. Whatever you did, change it: make it right again. After everything that happened, everything that you two have been through. Happy endings don't happen only in Bollywood movies, you know."

Sniffing away heavy mucus, Gorbind did his best to nod. He knew what he had to do, but first he would eat. His gut-sick feelings of despair had rather supressed his appetite. There was a deep, bass drum like grumbling from his gut. His grandmother must have heard it as she picked up the plated sandwiches and balance the dish on his knee.

"You eat this," Nani was making no bones about anything. "Drink your tea as well. I need to go make a 'phone call. Save me some biscuits," she tapped her own knees before hefting herself from the sofa. "I need some for the drama that comes on at half one, just after the news."

Doing as he was told, Gorbind picked up half a sandwich and nibbled at it. Nani was right.

He had to make this right.

CHAPTER 28

The door to the living room had been left ajar. The T.V. was still on, and he had polished off one of the three sandwiches that Nani had made. He could hear Nani's bangles jangle as she walked; her feet moved slowly and softly down the stairs.

Gorbind had counted four steps before Nani stopped moving.

"Padmi? Yes, it's Nani."

That immediately had his attention. Gorbind felt his hackles rise. He almost lurched from the sofa. His stomach was starting to churn again; he was convinced that he was about to throw up. Gorbind's shoulders sagged and slouched into the sofa.

Leaving the door open was all too deliberate. This, like everything else, he would have to endure. Gorbind only had himself to blame. No good would come from protesting.

"Beta, I know it hurts," Nani tutted, before listening further. He couldn't hear what Padmi might be saying; he would have to get up, go loiter by the door. The thought was as clear as a bell as it crossed his mind. Gorbind slid off the sofa, to take up stealthy sentry at the door.

"My grandson is an idiot," Nani was blunt, using a combination of nativised English and Punjabi. "His friend's wedding must've scared him; you were right about that, Beta."

"This is what he does," his grandmother was still going. "He gets scared, does something stupid. Then he sulks and makes everyone else miserable. When he was eighteen, he got drunk before his exams. Him and his friends ran half naked down the High Street and nearly got arrested. I had to ground him. Gorbind didn't speak to anyone for a week."

Pressing his ear to the door, he tried to listen. His grandmother did the same for the next minute and a half. All he could hear was the odd 'yes', 'no', and 'I know'. Not hearing Padmi's responses was ramping up his curiosity. This was killing him from the inside out.

"If I didn't love him, Padmi. If I didn't love you, beta, I wouldn't have called," Nani took in a deep breath, he heard her bangles clink. "Whatever he said, he won't have meant it. It's easier for him to lash out, than to try and understand. Yes, he's sat on the sofa with sandwiches. He must have called in sick to work, he never does that. What, you did that too?"

Trying to listen closely, Gorbind's forehead was kissing the door. If he were to move any closer, he would most likely brain himself.

"You are both miserable, because you are apart," Nani's tone started to change a little. "You two aren't meant to be apart. Any half-educated fool will tell you that. Padmi, you helped Gorbind feel happy again; helped him heal so that he could feel joy. When you're together, the both of you just glow. It's a light that is nothing short of heavenly."

A hair's breadth from the door, Gorbind heard Nani fall silent once more. She was listening, he was listening. This felt like the sword of Damocles, big time.

"I don't like hearing you both in pain, Beta," Nani broke the silence after what felt like an eternity. "You're two halves of one soul, Padmi. Together, you are strong. Together, you can take on anything. You, for one, took on Arjun. Not many sane people would do that, anyway. Then there is me, Padmi. You brought love and light back into my life when I thought I had lost it forever. You've made an old woman very happy. You've made my boys happy and that's a small miracle. Never mind them two, I don't want to lose you either."

Stuffing a damp piece of tissue into his mouth, Gorbind squeezed his eyes shut. He could imagine Nani's heart about crack straight down the middle.

"I need to go," Said Nani. "He's standing by the door; I can see his shadow across the floor. I've said my piece, Beta. You take care. Gorbind will make it right; he has to."

He heard the finalities of the conversation before Nani hung up. Gorbind nudged the door a little and scarpered back to the sofa. Crawling under his blanket, he feigned being asleep as Nani peered in and thumped the door closed.

To make it right, would hurt and then some.

CHAPTER 29

Gorbind eventually dozed off. The stack of sandwiches was slowly but surely demolished whilst his brains rotted with day-time television. Somewhere around tea-time, the doorbell rang, waking him up. This was followed by the living room door swinging sharply on its hinges to hit the wall.

"YOU JACKASS!" roared Arjun, striding in to loom over him. Dressed in a rather neatly tailored navy-coloured suit, he had no doubt clocked off early from work. "You dumped Padmi?! You, brother dearest, are a prized pillock," he said leaning in to jab his finger into Gorbind's shoulder. Arjun was several shades of incensed. His eyes bulged; there was a distinct pink tinge to them. Then there was the vein above his left eye that only ever appeared when he was truly enraged.

"You spoke to her?" Gorbind kicked away the blanket. He got to his feet to stand toe-to-toe with his brother.

"At length," nodded Arjun, his hands squarely on his hips. His nostrils flared, and Gorbind could see his knuckles whiten. "What the-are you insane?" curling his fingers, Arjun stepped back to pace across the room.

"She called me to say goodbye," he said, glowering at Gorbind as he turned on his heel. "Naturally, I jumped to conclusions; my radar went bat poop crazy. There's only room for one diva in this family," Arjun stretched out his long legs as he continued pacing. "You dumped her," he yelled, throwing his hands into the air with despair. "You got a dose of collywobbles with Davey's wedding. You got an idea of what you could have with Padmi, it scared you crapless. That, that makes you a grade A jack-ass."

Rooted to the spot, Gorbind had no idea when he had become so transparent to his family. Unable to respond, he sank back to the sofa with his elbows resting on his knees. He clutched his head in his hands and braced for the storm. Closing his eyes, he didn't want the pacing to make him feel any more disorientated.

"Straight-bloody-laced!" Arjun pivoted at the end of the room. "She told me everything, practically verbatim. Padmi held onto every single word as though you had branded her, Gorbind. You don't do crap like that, even I know that. You; you, genius," he wagged his finger again. It might as well have been a sabre. "Are meant to be the normal one, the one who has all the sense. The one takes everything in his stride; doesn't make a fuss, and baulks in the face of drama. The one who doesn't go 'round breaking young girls hearts."

Gorbind snapped his eyes open at the mention of the lyric. Arjun stopped pacing and landed heavily next to him on the sofa.

"I hope you feel like crap," Ajun spat out his words. "I hope that she find's someone worthy, someone who will treat her properly. Someone who doesn't get so bloody scared, bolt at the sound of a confetti canon. I hope that she finds someone who rings her wedding bells and then some. Well done, Gorbind, you did good there." Out of breath and sour faced, Arjun slumped back into the sofa.

Gorbind clamped his hands over his eyes. Arjun's diatribe had made him feel a thousand times worse.

Then the door-bell rang for the second time in half an hour.

Gorbind and Arjun both looked at one another.

"Gorbind!" yelled Nani. "If you don't open that front door, so help me-"

He had never moved so far. Arjun pulled him up from the sofa to throw him across the room. Gorbind travelled as fast as he could, hurtling towards the front door.

Arjun then made a swift exit into the kitchen, closing the door with a thud.

All fingers and thumbs, Gorbind did his best to open the door as quickly as he could. Flinging it back, he half tumbled out into his visitor.

Where he ended up, was on his knees in front of Padmi. She'd followed him to the ground, her arms unable to catch him.

Both of them faced each other, whilst kneeling on concrete littered with lilac petals.

"I got scared," said Gorbind, trying not to choke on tears and bogey.

"And did something stupid," Nodded Padmi, her arms had snaked around his torso. "You made me sulk, say goodbye to Arjun. You almost broke Nani's heart. Did Arjun tell you, tell you how much of a pillock and jackass you are?"

Gorbind nodded as he fiddled with the belt loops at her waist.

"I can't function without you," he said, spluttering and trying to catch his breath. "It's as though half of me is missing and it hurts. I'm half a human being; without you, Padmi, I am incomplete."

"I know," Padmi passed a palm across her cheek. "I woke up today, and you were the first person I thought about. All I wanted was for you to hug me. Not having that hug ever again, not being in your arms again. Gorbind, I couldn't breathe, I felt sick. I couldn't face going into work, being half a human being. Please don't do this again. Promise me, that you'll never do anything like this again."

Shuffling closer still, Gorbind ignored the throbbing of his knees on uneven concrete. All he could to stop himself from keeling over was to wrap his arms around her.

This was making it right; this was being a whole human being and not just half a heart.

Padmi was his whole world, his everything.

Letting her go, simply wasn't an option.

CHAPTER 30

"Padmi's not in," said Subash, stepping aside from the front door to let Gorbind in. "She's gone out with her mum."

"That's okay," replied Gorbind, wiping his feet as he stepped in. "It was you I wanted to see anyway," he added, closing the door behind him. "I was hoping to talk to you about something."

"Oh, yes?" asked Subash, "I'm about to stick the kettle on, come on through. We can talk in the kitchen."

Taking off his coat, Gorbind hung it off the end of staircase.

Subash was filling the kettle with freshly drawn water

as Gorbind arrived.

Unprompted, Gorbind plucked two black mugs from a metallic mug tree that sat by the microwave. He had done this so many times before that it was almost second nature. It was most definitely routine as Subash sat at the kitchen table. Dropping a teabag into one, he put two level teaspoons of coffee and an equal measure of brown sugar in the other.

Gorbind felt eyes watching him, and for the moment he avoided all eye contact. Clicking on the kettle on and off twice, he was more than a little anxious. He scuttled towards the 'fridge to pull out a bottle of skimmed milk and unscrewed the top in readiness. Placing it by the kettle, he silently willed the device to boil quicker.

"What's the matter, Gorbind?" Subash asked, fiddling with a salt and pepper set. "Since when did you come to see me and not my daughter? You look altogether a little twitchy. Spit it out, young man, it's not as though I'm going to eat you."

Putting his palms across the two mugs, Gorbind squeezed his eyes tight to steady himself. Somewhere in his stomach, a tornado of nausea-rather than the clichéd wave-was starting to churn. The click of a boiled kettle cued him to open his eyes, a white plume of vapour swirled from the spout. Picking it up, he filled each of the mugs. Out of the corner of his eye, he could see Subash studying him carefully. Putting the kettle back on its base, he stirred the black coffee and his own tea.

"I'm not getting any younger sat here waiting," Subash declared. "Don't put so much milk in my coffee. Not so keen on weak-willed coffee, it's a bit pointless."

Splashing the smallest amount of milk he could in it, Gorbind put the coffee down on the table. Pouring milk into his own tea, Gorbind left the teabag in and joined Subash at the table.

"All right," he said sitting down heavily. "I'll say it straight. I'd like your blessing," Gorbind blinked to focus. "To propose to Padmi; I want to ask her to marry me. So that we can be together properly, it's about time that we were."

Picking up his coffee, Subash took a mouthful. He didn't take his eyes of Gorbind; perhaps he was trying to determine the strength of the coffee rather than whether or not whether he should give Gorbind his blessing.

In defence, Gorbind picked up his tea. Picked up his tea to hide behind as he prayed; prayed that he wasn't about to be shot down. He must have eyeballed Subash for a good minute and a half across the top of his mug.

"Are you sure?" asked Subash, breaking the suffocating silence. "Only you look like a bunny rabbit in headlights. If you can't survive having a cuppa with me, how do you plan to cope with Padmi?"

"I can, I will," Gorbind stated firmly, sitting forward to lean on the table. "I've been there when she's been at her highest, caught her at her lowest. I have fought with her, for her; I have walked this far with her. I love her to her bones, would trade my soul to spend eternity with her. Woe betide anyone who would want to hurt Padmi, they would have to go through me. I won't give her up without a fight."

His heart was slowing down, the tornado in his stomach continued to spin. He wasn't done just yet.

"Padmi makes me a better man, a happier human being," he put down his mug next to the salt and pepper mill. "If I was to marry Padmi, she would keep it that way. She's the centre of my whole universe, and I want to build my world around her."

"You don't need my blessing then, do you," said Subash, also putting down his mug. "What you need to do is to ask Padmi, Ask her; tell her how much she means to you. That's all she wants, that's all that her mother and I want for her too. The pair of you belong together," he said nodding. "I'd be very proud to call you my son-in-law," his hand crept across the table, with fingers stretched out.

"I'll do it, I promise," Gorbind shook the proffered hand; he'd shaken on it. A deal was a deal. "I would sooner die than cause Padmi pain. I just hope she says yes."

Gorbind had the one blessing; there was another that he also desperately craved. He would have to run this passed Nani too. All of this and before he even got to asking Padmi. That was the one thing that terrified him completely. If, as Subash had said, he looked like a bunny in the headlights, then he had to get over it. He'd ask, hope that she said yes. Anything else really didn't bear thinking about.

CHAPTER 31

Turning the key in the door, Gorbind let himself in. He had already called his grandmother, telling her that he was on his way and bringing samosas. A white, plastic bag swung from his wrist. Inside, were piping hot samosas and half a pound of sticky, sweet Jalebis for afters.

"Gorbind?" Nani had heard him come in. She was in the lounge; he could hear the sound of an Indian telenovela with its rather bass-heavy sound track.

"Yeah, it's me," he replied, edging into the kitchen. There he dropped the carrier bag onto the work top and found some side plates. Opening up a brown paper bag that sat inside the carrier, he plated up two samosas. Taking the lid off a polystyrene cup, Gorbind poured a puddle of orange, carroty chutney next to the deep-fried pastries. There was just something about freshly made samosas that made his mouth water and his soul sing. Picking up the plates, Gorbind made his way into the living room.

"They still hot," asked Nani, looking at him over gold-rimmed glasses. Whilst the television was on, she had a set of knitting needles in her lap. Her current project was a deep maroon panel that would become either a scarf or a jumper. He himself had three different scarves hanging from his coat-stand. All being well, this would be another jumper for Arjun. Come rain or shine, Nani was convinced that Arjun was never dressed properly.

Nodding, Gorbind placed two plates onto the coffee table. Sitting down, he pulled the table closer towards them both.

Putting aside her knitting, Nani picked up a plate to put it on her lap. "Special day?" she asked, picking up a samosa. "Been a while since you last bought me samosas, Gorbind; there must a be good reason," she smiled a little, pushing her glasses up on the bridge of her nose.

"Sort of," he replied. "I went to see Padmi's dad. I had something to ask him. The same thing, I want to ask you, Nani."

Nibbling at the corner of the sofa, Nani looked

directly at him.

"I asked him for his blessing," Gorbind continued. "So that I can ask Padmi to marry me; I want to ask you for your blessing too." Breaking off eye contact, he picked up own plate to sit back on the sofa. He looked at the samosas, rather than at Nani. The pastries weren't as scary.

Still keeping his eyes down, he could see that Nani was still nibbling at her samosa. She kept silently nibbling for the next minute or so, until the whole samosa was gone. Gorbind could feel a breath forming a bubble in his throat; it was waiting for Nani to speak, so that it could pop.

"And what did he say, exactly?" asked Nani, he caught her blink as he finally looked up. Her brown-grey eyes focused upon him. "What did Subash say, about you marrying his daughter?"

Gorbind held onto his plate. There was just something about her tone that unnerved him. Something that threw him back into time, made him feel like a naughty ten-year old who had eaten chocolate before his dinner.

"That I should ask her," he replied, his two thumbs pressed against greasy, crumbly pastry of the samosa. "That Padmi also wants the same; that he would be very proud to call me his son-in-law. What about you,

Nani?" he asked, slowly looking up. "How would you feel about Padmi, being your granddaughter-in-law?"

He watched Nani move her plate onto the coffee table. He did the same. In his stomach, butterflies bounced around as they tried to head to his kidneys. Gorbind splayed his fingers across his knees.

"Ask her," Nani replied, moving her hand to place it on his. "When you needed a friend, she was there for you. When you were broken, Padmi put you back together far better than I and Arjun ever could. When you are together, you both shine with joy. You both fill this house with such joy, noise and love, it is beautiful. When you're apart, you are both so miserable; you'd think the moon had been shot down, things get that dark. Ask her, Gorbind. I give you my blessing with all of my love."

Unable to say anything, Gorbind lurched forward to throw his arms around Nani. He gave her the biggest bear-hug that he could muster. Blessing and love; that was all he needed. Job done.

CHAPTER 32

Standing over Arjun, Gorbind was removing hi-ball glasses from a cupboard. Somewhere near his knees, Arjun was looking for dinner plates and bowls. From the other side of the kitchen, Gorbind could hear Nani scrape pans with a ladle. There was an assortment of dishes that had been prepared for the evening's dinner; these were then decanted into glass serving bowls.

"Make sure you all tidy up," said Nani, turning a little to face them both whilst waving a ladle at them. It was smeared with green saag and bits of broken paneer. "I'm not washing up, so do it yourselves or stack the machine," tutting, she turned back to the pans. "Sheer laziness having a machine; why would I need one, there's only one of me," Nani was about to grumble for England.

"Only gets used when you kids are here. Arjun, take these bowls. PRIYA, AJIT!" Her yelling made the pans and glassware ring as she tapped at the window above the sink. "You two come here and help," she glared at her other grandchildren through the glass, beckoning them to come in.

Gorbind smiled as he closed the cupboard near his head; he then side-stepped his brother. "Nani, you forgot Rohan," he nodded at the window, just as she was about step back.

"ROHAN!"

Gorbind slunk passed, grimacing as he carried crockery. He headed out through the back door that had been left ajar. His route took him down a narrow alley lined with flagstones. It dog-legged left to come out at a neat square patio that sat beneath Nani's kitchen window. He placed the crockery onto a picnic table; a pulse of warm air drifted towards him from a blue-black Chiminea.

As Gorbind set the table, his cousins arrived with Arjun and bowls of food. He looked up briefly to catch sight of Arjun carrying a stack of hot, well buttered, fluffy chappatis encased in aluminium foil and tea-towels. He had made half of them, so he took a very particular interest as Arjun set the pile down onto the table.

When it came to family dinners, there was one very specific rule in Nani's kitchen. The boys would make the rotis, the girls were not allowed to so much as sniff the flour. Feminism had not entirely passed Nani by; she had trained him, Rohan too. Arjun was hopeless, he couldn't roll them 'round enough and recoiled at flipping them on the tava. His fingers were all too useful, apparently, to be burned to a crisp. Ajit, hid in the shadows and never tried anything.

Gorbind clambered onto the bench below the table as the last bowl was placed upon it.

Arjun and the cousins followed to fall in. Every couple of months, he, Arjun and the cousins would all descend upon Nani's. Here, they would convene for a catch up. More importantly, they would all check-in with their grandmother. If they didn't, there would be unavoidable, lengthy 'phone calls that involved each and every one of them being lectured on family values. Attendance was generally therefore, regular and healthy. Nani might have been stern at serving up, but she revelled in having a full house.

Holding out his hands, Gorbind received a stack of chappatis and removed the three that he planned to eat. The foil around the pile crackled as he passed them on and plated up his dinner.

"There's no salt in this," Priya declared, her nose wrinkling as she pointed her spoon at the saag-paneer that Gorbind had made.

"You burned the cauliflower," Arjun told Rohan, scooping up a couple of florets to plonk them on to his plate.

"Thank you for okra," Gorbind nodded at Priya; he was in no mood for her culinary criticism. "Yogurt again, Ajit," he shook his head at his cousin. "Never the hard stuff, eh?" teased Gorbind, knowing that Ajit had probably delegated this to his wife Roshni to avoid making an effort. He caught Ajit glaring at him whilst Gorbind tore up chappatis.

"You're welcome," acknowledged Priya. "This has all turned out lovely. However, what I really want to know, is what are you doing with Padmi, exactly?" she elbowed Ajit to sit forward a little.

Concentrating on his dinner, Gorbind nonchalantly shrugged his shoulders. He could feel all three of them eyeballing him; the shrug was a figurative two-fingers that really didn't cut it.

"Get a wiggle on, would you," continued Priya, her spoon waggled once more. "You need to hurry up, ask her to marry you. I got tired of waiting for Aran to pop the question, so I did it myself. All he has to do is provide the sparkly piece of rock," she was smirking by now. "Or do I have to give Padmi some sisterly advice, some encouragement to take matters into her own hands."

"Don't you dare," Gorbind snapped his eyes toward Priya. "I will ask her, I want to; I just haven't figured the how and when."

"Muppet," muttered Arjun, stuffing his mouth with food.

Ajit and Rohan exchanged quizzical looks across the table.

"You've known her, what four-five years," started Rohan. "And you've not figured it out yet?" he asked, his eyes narrowing with curiosity.

"He's shafted," sighed Ajit. "Let her do it, tell her," he nodded towards Priya. "Encourage her. Gorbind has all the boy bits of a wet haddock. Padmi can help you gain some proper. You've done the hard bit, the traditional bit; asking her dad and all that. What's the matter with you?" he asked, tearing a chappati in half. "Jackass. Priya's right. You can't keep her hanging like this."

Letting his shoulders sag, Gorbind felt and looked downcast. ""I'm bloody petrified," he muttered; his words were barely audible.

Reaching over, Priya rapped his knuckles with a ladle.

"Say that again, sunshine," she demanded, cupping an ear with her palm. "I don't think I heard you. Padmi never will either, by the sound of things."

Snatching his hand back, Gorbind's snapped his shoulders straight. "I said I'm petrified, that I'm quite literally bricking it," he made no apologies for sounding terse. "I haven't even told her about the training course for the 'force yet. She doesn't know yet, about my application going through successfully. This, and with that; which do I first, exactly?" he asked, waving his hands around. "I don't know which scares me more. Being a husband or getting through the course at Ryton. I love Padmi, she's amazing."

Letting out a deep, constrained breath, he rolled his shoulders. "My world is bigger, better with her in it. Getting through Ryton, being part of the 'force. I want both, both scare the life out of me in equal measure. Ryton will probably break me physically, but Padmi could do it emotionally. If she says no; then yes, as Ajit says, I will shafted." He looked searchingly around the table, hoping that one of them would rescue him, take away the limelight that had been forced upon him.

Priya rolled her eyes, tutting sharply. "She's put up with you all these years," she said putting more okra to her plate. "Nani has met her, Arjun reckons that she's Aphrodite incarnate. You, Gorbind, can't breathe without her. Grow a set!" she pronounced, once more rapping his knuckles. "Do both; be the good husband, get through Ryton. You managed to get through Uni with flying colours and you are sick of number crunching all day. Take the flaming plunge.

"Wet haddock," coughed Ajit, a fist held before his mouth.

"Do it," nodded Rohan. "Feel the fear, mate, do it anyway. Stop dilly-dallying."

Put in his pace, Gorbind ate his dinner like a sullen child. He'd been told in no uncertain terms what he had to do. His mind was a jumble as to how to do it. In the meantime, Priya was right. There really wasn't enough salt in the saag-paneer.

CHAPTER 33

"Gorbind, open this door! I know you're in there. Open this door, or so help me, Lord, I will cause a scene in the street."

Gorbind was jolted awake; he tumbled sideways off the sofa to land onto the floor. Heavy blows rained against the door of number 28 Acacia Avenue. The doorbell also being rang incessantly, drowning out the sound of some mundane soap opera on the television.

Landing on all fours, Gorbind crawled towards the hallway. He got to his feet as he exited the lounge. Gorbind remembered coming home from the gym and falling asleep on the sofa; his hair was still a little damp as he ran his fingers through the locks and backwards against his scalp.

He knew that voice; it was crystal clear to whom it belonged. The last he had heard it, the tones has been sweet and gentle. Now, not so much; now the voice was shrill and bordering on incandescent. At this very moment, the voice of his beloved sounded somewhere between a depraved banshee and a grenade going off.

"Open the door."

Still there were kicks, thumping too. The door vibrated with the forced being used to pummel it. He raised a brow at the rattling of the letter box.

Puffing out his cheeks, Gorbind asked the universe for strength. He counted to three and then-

"WHAT?!" roared Gorbind, pulling the door open. He stood toe to toe with Padmi. "WHAT ON EARTH IS WRONG-"

He was unable to get anymore words out; Padmi had charged forwards. She looked like woman possessed as she hurtled indoors with her arm raised ready to deck him one.

"You need to make your mind up, hic," screeched Padmi. "Where is this going? We've had years of messing around. Do you even think about getting married? I'm not wasting any more time waiting for you stop pratting around, for you to do the right thing. I am tired, Gorbind," her arms were gesticulating wildly. In his head, she looked like an ostrich trying to take off. That was probably something to keep to himself. "I am not putting my life on hold, just because you have no clue what the flip to do with your own."

She edged closer towards him, shoulders held high and fists hanging at her sides.

As Padmi moved, he caught the scent. The scent of alcohol-several different types-there was sticky, sweet bourbon as well as fruity wine that Gorbind never had any time for.

He winced as Padmi pivoted; she slammed the door shut behind her. Her palm landed heavily on his shoulder as she pushed him backwards down the hall. Padmi's eyes were completely glazed over, horribly pink too.

Padmi pushed him through the closed living room door she continued to rant. Gorbind had no time to protest as he was propelled backwards still.

"This, this is an ultimatum," Padmi waggled a finger, before trying to push Gorbind down onto the sofa; only she missed. "You and I, we need to talk," her eyes narrowed, suggesting that she was trying focus as she started to sway. "What is happening here, you need to tell me."

Grasping a hold of her finger, Gorbind put his other

hand to her waist. Taking her into his arms, he rotated Padmi one hundred and eighty degrees to haul her onto the sofa. Sat her next to her, he held his hands in hers. He didn't trust her not to try and smack him one.

"Good night with the girls was it?" he asked, briefly looking at the watch on his wrist. It was only just midnight. All things considered, the night was still young. It was very early for Padmi to be this drunk already. "Thought you'd be out til early in the morning," he offered. "That I wasn't going to see you for a couple of days." Gorbind kept his tone level, despite trying to not laugh. He had never seen or heard Padmi this rip-roaring drunk before. This particular level of inebriation was an entirely new thing to wrap his head around; what he needed to do was trust his intuition and go with it.

"They're still going," she spat out the words, as her face flushed pink. "All I could do was think about you, so I told them about you. I told them about your dilly-dallying." The finger was back, waggling with full force having escaped his hold.

"That's lovely," nodded Gorbind. "Very sweet, but you are this hammered because?"

"Because I told them about how you won't commit," slurred Padmi. "That perhaps you don't want to," she moved her finger, poked him repeatedly in the stomach before kicking off her heels in the direction of the fire place.

"Hey, stop that," he slid back from the finger a little. "What, why, when did I say any of that?" squeaked Gorbind as Padmi let out a very dramatic sigh. Having given up assaulting him with an inoffensive weapon, she was now curling up around him.

Only something didn't feel right as she held him in a vice like grip.

"Gorbind," his name came out garbled. Her body was vibrating against his and not in a nice way.

Carrying her to the kitchen, he made sure that Padmi didn't fall into the sink as bourbon and wine made an unwelcome reappearance.

CHAPTER 34

"What time is it?" Padmi yawned, holding a palm flat across her mouth. There was still some lack of hand-eye co-ordination as she more or less slapped herself across the face.

"Half one," replied Gorbind, he too yawned. He hadn't anticipated his night-in being interrupted or being awake til the early hours. Somehow, he had managed to get Padmi upstairs and into bed. Twice they had nearly fallen down the narrow flight of stairs as Padmi had continued to wrestle with him whilst in the throes of a drunken stupor.

It was far more difficult to climb the stairs when she almost paralytic. When she was sober, Padmi took no time at all to haul him up the wooden hill. Whilst they didn't live together, she knew her way both up and down the stairs relatively well; just not at that moment in time. Padmi would spend most weekends here with Gorbind, in this two up, two down. When she was here, the house didn't feel so empty, so big and it was never quiet. She had been here when he had got the keys; she'd helped to decorate so that the house didn't become one great big man-cave.

"Here, drink this," He kept his arm coiled around her as he leant across to pick up a pint glass of water that was sat on her bed-side cabinet. There was also a blister pack of paracetamol with two tablets missing.

"Slowly," he whispered as Padmi drank with her fingers tips clutching the glass. "This is going to hurt in the morning. Oh, look, you've hurt your hands too," he couldn't help but tut as he traced a thumb across the back of her scuffed, scratched hands. "Trying to break my door down wasn't one of your brightest ideas, now was it? As lovely as I am, the door really isn't worth it." He settled back against cushions to hold his hand against his forehead. He was starting to wilt, big time.

"And I'm annoyed," continued Gorbind. "You went off on one with the girls, told them that I wasn't going to commit." He could hear a hurt, irritated burr in his words; no part of it was assuaged away as Padmi plonked a warm foot across his knee. His ankle twitched as reflex kicked in. She had a tendency to drag her toes across his legs she did that right now as she dozed with her eyes closed.

"Dent bey," said Padmi, her return to sobriety was not happening quickly. "Step beying 'noyed. Jest maree mey enstead."

Gorbind had been half listening; the mutterings of drunken women had always rather passed him by. This level of Drunken Padmi was still very new to him; he had no idea how to interpret what she was saying. He took a few moments to process what she had just uttered.

"Did you hear me?" Padmi asked, shuffling away to put her glass back before sliding back to the middle of the bed.

He had frozen, one arm held out as she left his orbit. In his head, this was not the way it was supposed to go. If there was going to be a proposal, he figured that he'd be the one making it. His face was about to give him away; his lips had parted as though to protest. Gorbind's brows arched as he looked aghast.

"Gorbind, marry me," Padmi pulled him upright into a seated position. With the other curled into a fist, she rubbed her eye. She blinked, focused and set her weary gaze upon him. "For the love of God, don't leave me hanging. This isn't fair. Say something."

"I wanted to ask you," he finally uttered. "Hanging?" Gorbind asked, pointedly as he gathered up his legs.

"No one is hanging. I'm not keeping you hanging. God, Padmi, I have no idea what is going on." He slumped into the folds of the duvet that they shared, held his head in his hands and looked at her through splayed fingers.

Padmi inclined her head to the side and looked as though she was trying to concentrate.

That, Gorbind, figured, or she was trying not to be sick again. He hoped that she wouldn't be sick again as they sat in silence for what seemed to be forever.

"Yes," he said after a while; still he looked at her through his fingers. "But can we do this again? I want a chance to ask you, ask you properly."

"Screw that," screamed Padmi, lurching forward. Her arm engulfing him entirely; once more Padmi clamped him close. "You said yes. You bloody well said yes."

Thrown backwards, he almost hit his head off the wall as Padmi pinned him in place. Unable to move, Gorbind offered no resistance as the woman he loved sobered up rather quickly. She had sobered up, to make short work of liberating him from his pyjama bottoms and then some.

It was half four by the time they had finished celebrating their new engagement. Gorbind kicked himself as he uncurled himself from Padmi's arms as she fell asleep. Kicked himself for having dilly-dallied, kicked himself for having already asked her father for her hand only not to do anything about it. Not once had he foreseen being pipped to the post. Turning on his side, Gorbind sulked for a while; he plotted his next move.

Gorbind would ask. She could take away his sanity; take eighty per cent of his duvet. He would propose and at least he would be sober. Bourbon combined white wine really weren't his thing.

CHAPTER 35

"What you trying to do exactly?" Arjun asked, raising half a pint to his lips. "It'll get very warm before you break it with your magic mind bullets or Jedi super powers what have you."

Gorbind's thoughts went poof and fizzled away.

For the last half an hour, he had been sat here with Arjun who was yammering on. All he could think about was Padmi's drunken proposal as he looked at his beer with its frothy, bubbling head. It had been three days since he and Padmi were last together. There had been a smattering of messages, awkward telephone conversations filling the gap. He was reeling still at being ambushed, at not being quick enough to propose. Gorbind felt stupidly sore at being outpaced.

He should have listened to Rohan; he should have stopped dilly-dallying well before Padmi had got in so quick.

Pressing his lips together, he bit away dry, chapped skin and picked up his glass. Gorbind took a mouthful; Arjun was right, the beer was now a little warm. He gulped it down regardless.

"Padmi proposed," he said speaking over the froth-edged rim of the glass. "I said yes," he blinked, half held his breath and waited for a response.

Arjun blinked too; they had mirrored each other in both taking a slug of their beers. His glass moved aside, his mouth was agape.

"I wanted to do it," hissed Gorbind. "I was going to ask her; just couldn't figure out whether I should tell her about Ryton or vice versa. I was going to ask, she beat me to it," he thumped his glass down onto a brightly coloured, gaudy beer-mat. The impact dislodged some of the pale ale; it danced over the rim to trickle down to the beer-mat. "Padmi proposed."

"And you said yes," nodded Arjun. "I got all that, yes, I'm with you. Congratulations," he planted his drink down to grin like the Cheshire cat before crossing his arms over his grey, hooded sweatshirt. "I love Padmi, she's awesome," declared Arjun. "She got you to smarten up, look lively. I'm glad we get to keep her.

So what if she proposed," he shrugged nonchalantly to take another slug of his beer. "This isn't the seventeenth century, now is it? Serves you right for dilly-dallying," Arjun waggled a finger over his glass. "Rohan did tell you. He was bang on the money."

"Not having it," Gorbind gurned, shaking his head. "I'm going to do it; do it my way. I won't be half drunk or in a strop like she was."

Arjun sat forwards, laughing as he spluttered; his smoker's cough kicked in. He looked a little undignified as he tried not to choke.

"Which bit are you sore about, exactly?" he asked, giggling quietly. "The proposal that she robbed you of; the fact that she was half cut when she did it. Padmi saved you a job for crying out loud. Get over it," he said emphatically, draining his glass. "Another one?" he posed, pointing at Gorbind's glass.

"A half," replied Gorbind, tilting his head slightly. "I'm meant to meet her after work. She'll kill me if I'm hammered."

"Oh, the irony," muttered Arjun as he headed towards the bar.

Slurping what remained of his beer, Gorbind tried to focus. He would get his proposal, with bells on if necessary. All he needed was a plan, a fool proof one at that.

CHAPTER 36

This had better work," Gorbind slapped both his palms to his face, he needed to focus. "If it doesn't, you can have my soul with bells on, alright?" Ahead of him was Jacob Epstein's sculpture of the light-bringer.

"I came to see you first," he continued, passing a finger over his chapped lips. "I am in dire need of courage. You are after all, the Morningstar, the bringer of light and banisher of dark. Oh," he rubbed his eyes hard, and looked around furtively. It was only just ten o'clock; the gallery was quiet, yet to fill up. He was alone, apart from a red polo-shirted guide that was headed in the direction of the Staffordshire hoard.

"I must look half mad," he told the statue. "Standing

here, having a conversation with The Devil. Enough," he said shaking his head. "I need to go find Persephone. As you were, Morningstar. This might involve going to hell in a handbasket. Save me a room with a view, if you don't mind."

Slinking his hands into pockets of his chestnut-coloured duffle coat, Gorbind edged around Lucifer's raised platform. He shuffled slowly at first, eventually quickening his pace to head towards the Pre-Raphaelites. Gorbind gulped silently; his throat was drying up as his anxiety heightened.

He knew that particular gallery well; the blonde, wooden floor, the teal walls never seemed to lose their lustre. The walls had always felt protective against all of the heartbreak that he had experienced beyond the gallery. As he arrived at the gallery, Gorbind played the last conversation that he had with Padmi in his head.

"I need to find a new coat," he had said. "I'll be in town in the morning. Come find me, you get first refusal on the one that I buy."

"Could do," Padmi had replied. "I need a new dress for a hen do. If I don't veto your dodgy duffle, promise not to huff and puff with my dress?"

He had laughed wickedly. "I quite enjoy huffing and puffing at your dresses," he had got temporarily distracted imagining it. "Makes for interesting date nights, so please don't get one with too many zips and buttons. The damned things do rather get in my way."

Padmi had groaned across the line, he could picture her rolling her eyes. "So very droll. When and where?" Padmi had sounded as though she was checking for a spot in her diary.

"Persephone," he had replied. "Say a quarter past, half past ten. I'll even get lunch later," he offered by way of inducement.

He had then heard Padmi tut. "Flipping Persephone," she huffed. "You and that flaming museum! Okay, fine. Half past ten, you had better be worth it. I'm giving up my Saturday morning lie in for you, sunshine."

Gorbind had promised; promised that he was worth it, sent a splodgy kiss across the line before he hung up.

Shuffling toward Persephone, he glanced at his watch. There was still another ten minutes for their rendezvous. He knew Padmi's time keeping. She would get here as close to half past as she humanly could. Padmi liked to arrive on time; just in time, that was. Tucking his hands back into his pockets, Gorbind paced around the gallery. He eye balled Madaea, passing a his thumb across the top of a fuzzy box that was nestled against faux sheepskin lining. He must have walked passed Machiavellian Madaea at least eight times before he turned on his heel and saw her.

It was ten twenty-seven exactly. Gorbind double-checked his watch. Edging towards the portrait of Persephone, he still had his hands deep in his pockets. Fiddling with the lining helped reduce the nervous anxiety swirling around somewhere near his spleen.

Padmi was moving slowly towards him; it all felt very cinematic.

His brows knitted together as he realised the Padmi would make him wait the whole of the three remaining minutes. This was her idea of being on time. Three minutes that seemed to defy the laws of Physics and stretch into to an eternity.

The gallery blurred away around her; all he saw was Padmi. The sound of her heels clip-clopping across the floor heralded her arrival, mirroring the racing of his pulse. Gorbind moved his gaze across her instep, along black leather boots that stopped at her knees; beyond that were navy jeans. A baby pink jumper was only just visible beneath a tailored, dark-chocolate coloured coat that was tied against a narrow waist. Her waist; he knew that waist better than he would ever confess.

The way in which Padmi curved in and out in all the right places made for interesting lazy afternoons and warmer autumn mornings. Her dark locks-very subtly tinted at the roots; he would have to report that this was lovely-cascaded down toward her shoulders. There was a slight kink where her hair met with her shoulders that straighteners were never able to iron out. If all that remained of Padmi was her long, silken tresses, her vapid grin and her sparkling eyes, he would have the world on a string, and proclaim himself king. Gorbind knew exactly how to turn that vapid grin into an alluring smirk. He could stay lost in her eyes for ever and a day.

"Gorbind, you okay?" Padmi asked, she was in touching distance and put her hand to one of his toggles. "You've gone all doe-eyed and dreamy. Migraine?" there was a tone of concern that edged her voice.

"Seeing stars," whispered Gorbind, trying not to go cross-eyed as he fixed his gaze upon her. There was, after all, a significant height difference between them.

"Stars?" she asked, eyelashes fluttering as she looked a bit confused.

"Galaxies," said Gorbind, looming over to plunder a kiss. He let it permeate into every inch of his being. Drawing her close, he wrapped his arms around her waist. He tipped Padmi a little off balance, off her feet and into his arms. Padmi falling into his arms was never just a fantasy; when it happened, Gorbind enjoyed every moment of it.

He kept his feet firmly on the floor, with every inch of Padmi exactly where he wanted her. Given how hard her hands were clinging onto his shoulder blades, he figured that they had come to a mutual agreement.

"You don't need a new coat, do you?" Padmi's lips parted from his, they were both able to get some air.

"Not really, no," replied Gorbind, shaking his head. "What I want is you."

"Here in the museum?" She pulled back a little; her face had gone from pleasure to poker in about two seconds flat.

"Well," Gorbind stepped back too, rolling his shoulders a little but also keeping a hold of her hand. With the other, he delved into his pocket. "Hold that thought, for just a second," he said, sliding his foot back to slowly make his way to one knee.

Gorbind flipped open the lid of the box that had been sat his pocket. Sat nestled upon blue satin was a ring. A white gold band, set with two diamonds either side of an inky-blue sapphire.

"Here in the museum," he said softly. "Whilst we are

skating on thin ice, walking down Brighton pier, in sickness and in health. Where ever you want me, Padmi, I am all yours. If you will have me, I am yours permanently, for ever and a day. Marry me, Padmi."

All he could see was Padmi's very startled expression. Gorbind was trying not keel over. He felt all too vulnerable with her standing over him.

"Get up here and catch me," she stuttered. "I'm about to fall over, earn your answer."

Gorbind jolted to his feet as Padmi lurched forwards into his arms. As well as her laboured breathing, he could also hear a smattering of applause. She was clinging onto him for dear life with her face buried into his chest. Pressed against the base of her spine was the box; he was trying not to drop it.

"Forever is good," he heard her say. "I like permanent," she was sniffling away; there was probably a patch of bogey forming on his coat. "I've seen your sickness and your health, Gorbind."

"That a yes?" he asked, trying to tease the ring from the box.

Pulling away from the depths of his embrace, Padmi nodded. She passed a palm across the hollows of eyes, smudging eyeliner in the process. "It's a yes," she declared, holding our her hand, "And with bells on. Jesus, Gorbind, this took you long enough."

Rolling his eyes, Gorbind took her trembling hand to slide on the ring. He tucked it close to her knuckle, making sure that it was well and truly wedged on. Hades only had Persephone was six months. Gorbind had Padmi forever.

CHAPTER 37

Salt and Citrus; those were the distinct fragrances that hit Gorbind's nose as he turned his key in the door. A salty, bitterness was the top note that crowned the base note of zingy lemons. He should have known really. A couple of days ago, Nani had disclosed her plans to make lemon pickle. As he ushered Padmi on ahead down the corridor, he could hear the sharp clink of Nani's bangles against glass.

"Naniji, you in?" Padmi called out, pushing open the living room door.

Gorbind hung back a little; a ball of anxiety spun around in his chest to square up to his fast beating heart.

"Padmi, Beta, that you? Yes, you come in, beta," Nani

replied.

As they both entered, Gorbind saw Nani lift a blue and white, checked tea-towel from her lap and drop it onto a tray of quartered lemons. Lemons that Nani had asked him get from the fruit and veg market in town. He had brought an entire box; you could never have enough lemon pickle. His plan was to pinch a jar of pickle when she wasn't looking and stash it in his pantry. Sat next to the tray were two glass jars. One of them was already a third full with lemons layered with salt. His chest was feeling increasingly tight as Nani threw her arms around Padmi to hug her close.

"Please tell me that you said yes," Nani fumbled around with her scarf trying to reach Padmi's hands. Gorbind knew exactly what she was looking for. "I hope you said yes," Nani laughed as she finally found Padmi's left hand.

"I did, yes," nodded Padmi, stretching out her fingers. Sat on her wedding finger was a white gold band set with two square cut diamonds that sandwiched either side of an inky-blue sapphire.

"And I got Jalebis!" Gorbind declared, finally pipping up. He waved a small, red box. "You're the first to know, Nani. Want me to stick the kettle on?"

His grandmother waved a hand at him dismissively.

"In a minute," she said, tugging Padmi towards the sofa. "Give them here. Go up to my room; bring me the blue box from my dressing table."

Handing over the box, Gorbind did as he was told. He was however, wary of being sent off on a mission and abandoning his fiancé. He traipsed up the thick, beige coloured carpet of the stairs and into the master bedroom. The door had been left wide open, to make sure that he could see the dressing-table. A dark blue velveteen box sat squarely in the middle

Gorbind wasn't looking where he was going as he collided with the edge of the bed. "Balls," he exclaimed, air whistled over his teeth as he winced. Hobbling towards the table, he scooped up the box and turned heel as fast as he could. His calf protested as he thundered back down the stairs. He was curious about the box, it felt seriously important.

Back in the living room, Gorbind handed over the box before sitting down next to Padmi. She'd been put to work; lemon segments were being thrown into the glass jars and layered with more salt. He paid attention, seeing as one of them could be his.

"He wants one," Nani told Padmi as her fingers fiddled with the gold-coloured metal clasp of the velveteen box. "He thinks I don't know, about his plans to steal one; but I do. He can take that one," she said nodding to the one that Padmi had half filled.

"Put more salt in and don't forget the peppercorns." A whole heap of black-grey peppercorns sat nearby in a stainless steel bowl.

"I do," Gorbind grinned, reaching across and picking up a segment. Holding it beneath his nose, he inhaled deeply. "Nani's pickle is second to none. It goes beautifully with parathas."

"He does make his own parathas," said Nani, the box in her lap thudded open. "Padmi, these are for you, beta. I need to tell you something," she slid the box across her knees and onto Padmi's.

Gorbind felt his heart thud one huge beat, his stomach flipped too as the contents of the box were exposed. Resting in faux satin were two yellow-gold bracelets set with what looked like garnets in a filigree fretwork. He knew those bangles, the Kangana. He remembered seeing them at his mother's wrists when he was a child.

Biting his lip, Gorbind blinked back hot tears that had spontaneously started to form. He gulped down a sob as Padmi's fingers curled around his trembling hand. As she put her fingers to his, the shaking ebbed away.

"Gorbind might have bought you a ring, a very pretty ring," said Nani quietly. "But his mum left these for you. I gave them to her when she got married. If either one of the boys had been a girl, they would have been given these in their trousseau," she sighed gently, as a tear travelled down her cheek. "Gorbind came, Arjun too. You are the closest she would have had to a daughter, Padmi. It is only right that they go to you. These are a sagan, an engagement gift for you, to welcome you into the family properly."

He could see Padmi's bottom lip start to tremble; his was about to do the same. The ball of anxiety in his chest had exploded, smearing pure joy across his heart.

"I don't need to look after the boys anymore," said Nani, placing a palm gently to Padmi's face. "I've done everything that I could do, everything that needed to be done. It gives me great joy to hand Gorbind over to you. I know that you're a good woman, that you will love him, keep him safe and make sure that he stays happy. Padmi, he is all yours; every single bit of him."

Letting out a gasp, Gorbind passed a sleeve over his nose. He was gone, there was bogey everywhere. Being stoic, having a stiff upper lip had well and truly gone out the window.s

"Don't want his beard though," Padmi was also sobbing by now as Nani enveloped her in a hug.

"Especially his beard," laughed Nani, drying Padmi's tears with the end of her pale, lavender coloured scarf. "It's better than his feet."

Padmi nodded in agreement, half laughing, and half crying.

The two most important women in his life were happy, so was he.

CHAPTER 38

This was phase one of the whole getting married thing. There has been so many hoops to jump through, just to get this far. Gorbind had asked Subash for his daughter's hand; that had been one item. He had then dilly-dallied about how to actually do the deed, only for Padmi to ask him. That had left him feeling altogether hard done by. Some part of him was a still a little bit sore about that.

'*Your own fault,*' he told himself as he tugged down his shirt to draw breath.

'*If you hadn't bottled it, if you had just asked her. She perhaps wouldn't have popped the question,*' mused Gorbind. '*I don't mind feminism; just getting pipped to the bloody post.*'

He made sure that Arjun was standing next to him to

on his right. That was where he was supposed to be as his best-man.

In theory, Padmi had proposed and they had been engaged from there on in. Only he had actually wanted to ask, for his own selfish benefit. Gorbind had wanted to pop the question and with his own mouth. So he did; with rocks forged by mother earth over millennia. Each one was shiny, sparkly and had done the job superbly.

All that to-ing and fro-ing; so that he could be stood here in a tent on a wet Sunday afternoon making sure that he and Padmi were together properly. This wouldn't be the first time either. Phase two wouldn't happen for another two weeks. Today was about the legal formalities. He and Padmi would say 'I do' for the necessary bits and paper without any mention of religion; that would happen next time.

This was the white wedding that Padmi had dreamt about having since she was a little girl. Phase two would be vibrant vermillion and very different. Phase two was more in line what Gorbind wanted; he had waited years, two more weeks would nothing.

Out of the corner of his eye, Gorbind saw that Arjun had started to drift away from him. Landing a hand to his brother's shoulder, Gorbind curled his fingers to drag Arjun back into place.

"Stay where you are, Arjun," said Gorbind, he brushed raindrops from Arjun's shoulders, smoothing down the aubergine coloured fabric of his tuxedo. "I need you to stay still, stay upright for at least fifteen minutes. Give me the rings when you're asked, then you can keel over, crawl away as quickly as you want."

Gorbind gulped away spit balls of anxiety that had travelled up to his throat; he then fiddled with his own jacket. Making sure his buttons were done, he pressed a palm to his stomach. His jacket was a proper, well-tailored dinner jacket worn over a red shirt. He even had had bow-tie at his neck that twinkled in the light of chandeliers that were suspended from the ceiling. Matching his shirt, there were garnet cuff-links at his wrist. Cuff-links that had been a Christmas present years ago. Padmi had asked that he wear them today.

Arjun glared back at him, but fell in without argument.

The both of them had slipped out of Gorbind's house late the previous night for a swift half. It was half five and a few swift halves before they returned. This didn't leave them a lot of time, but they had somehow managed to sober up and get some sleep before having to suit up.

Behind them, one hundred of his and Padmi's nearest and dearest were gathered to witness the ceremony.

Rows of seating were arranged in a semi-circle, giving the tent something of a theatrical feel. The rows were bisected by a red carpet that connected the front of the tent to the entrance at the back; an entrance that was framed by an archway of silken roses and dark green foliage. Gorbind, with Arjun and the registrar, stood beneath red fabric that formed a canopy stretched between four posts. The posts were festooned with twinkling fairy lights as well as more faux red and white roses.

Once the vows were done, the canopy would give way to a DJ and an illuminated dance floor. The guests would be shooed off into the stately home that had been hired for today, where they would get refreshments as he and Padmi departed for photographs. They would return for the wedding breakfast, followed by their first dance. Beyond that, there was a plan to party til midnight. Everything was planned to go like clock-work. Padmi had left nothing to chance. Gorbind had heard the whole plan more times than he cared to remember.

Gorbind could feel his heart race. If it beat any faster, there was a small danger that it might pop and cause him to keel over into a heap. He thought it had when he heard drumming.

Hearing the rhythmic beat, Gorbind turned on the spot to see a traditionally-dressed drummer playing at the entrance of the tent. The drum suspended in front of him was beating beaten furiously. The drummer's eyes looked to be almost closed as he started to move towards the canopy and heralded the arrival of the bride.

The entrance of the tent parted.

There she was.

As Gorbind set his his eyes on his wife-to-be, he couldn't breathe.

Padmi had taken his breath away. His knees felt momentarily weak. Gorbind could feel himself start to sway. Perhaps he was about to drop; Arjun's palms landed sharply against his shoulder blades to keep him from falling.

To the innocent bystander, Gorbind appeared to rock a little on his heels.

He rocked enough to regain his centre of mass and be pulled back into the tent.

Accompanied by her father, Padmi travelled down the aisle in a white, fish-tailed gown. As the lights were dimmed, she appeared to be bathed in a glow that made the crystals on her dress shimmer. A string of red garnets glimmered at her neckline. These matched her deep red veil that was trimmed with even more crystals and snaked down towards the back of her knees. Padmi's usually straight hair had been curled into ringlets that bounced about her shoulders. In her hands was a bouquet of fresh, white roses.

Gorbind had been lost; lost in watching Padmi edge forward to arrive at the canopy. His reverie was broken by Arjun elbowing him, shoving him forward to meet her. He stumbled forward and eventually ended up standing almost face to face with his bride before the registrar. Puffing out his cheeks, Gorbind did his best to ground himself.

Padmi handed her bouquet to a bridesmaid to take both his hands.

They both shuffled closer towards each other.

He laughed nervously, as he loomed over her; she had good view up his nose. Drawing in breath, he caught her wink at him. Her hands were actually very warm, but there was coldness beneath his fingers that came from her engagement ring.

He had her hands, she had his heart.

Gorbind kept his eyes front and centre as the registrar started making her declarations. Arjun had the rings; his vows were in Gorbind's own breast pocket.

With his heart in her hands, Gorbind was giving away his whole world. Padmi was the centre of his universe; this was more than a fair exchange. Anything that happened after today would only make it bigger, better and stronger.

CHAPTER 39

Today, he was getting married. He was getting married *again*. The thought burst across Gorbind's mind causing him to wake. The second bedroom here at Nani's was shrouded with a grey darkness; so much so that he went almost cross-eyed as he tried to focus on the spherical lampshade suspended from the ceiling rose.

The last that Gorbind remembered was being hauled up here by his brother at half two in the morning. Somehow, he had landed in his bed to be submerged beneath a fifteen tog, red and grey striped duvet that now saw somewhat heavily across his shoulders. Events leading up to that were somewhat blurry. There was a noisy memory that echoed with drums and a whole lot of bass.

"You awake?" asked a disembodied voice a short distance away.

An arm followed the question; a wrist flicked forward as fingers groped searchingly around on the duvet.

"Yes," replied Gorbind, almost growling. The hand had landed with slap across the bridge of his nose. Moving his face, he grasped a hold of the offending article. An article that smelt oddly of white musk soap, he flung the fingers back towards their owner. Turning on his side, Gorbind gathered his duvet up around him, tucking an edge below his chin. He peered through the darkness to look at his brother.

"Did you even sleep?" Queried Gorbind, there was a tone of incredulity to his voice. "Bloody hell, you slept down there?" he leant forward a little to see that Arjun's bed was on the floor next to his. He slid back and tutted whilst rubbing his eye with the heel of his left hand.

"A little bit," replied Arjun. He shuffled a little, there was a soft huff from the blow up mattress that he slept on. It was covered in a pale blue sheet that only just covered it and a matching navy duvet that looked far lumpier than Gorbind's. "It was sleep here," he continued yawning, "Or bunk up on the sofa before getting woken up by Nani doing her morning Paath."

As if on cue, Gorbind heard the muffled strains of

Ardas being played downstairs. There was just something about the way the harmonium and tabla combined to stir the soul.

"Plus," Arjun still wasn't done as he blinked several times. "As your best man, I'm supposed to keep an eye on you at all times. Nani said so," he arched a brow to give his brother something of a vapid grin.

"Did she really?" Gorbind's sing song tone was glazed with disbelief. He couldn't but help but laugh as he scratched the dark stubble that was a fuzzy mass across his jawline. It had taken weeks to get to its current density. He wasn't quite a pirate, but he wasn't about to become a Hell's Angel either.

"I'm not exactly going to go running, now am I? Can't believe she's up already either," Gorbind puffed out his cheeks to blow out stale morning breath. "We came up at half two; it was Nani that hauled us out of the friggin' tent. Half bloody two. What time is it now, bud. Five, six?"

"Hold on," Arjun shuffled on his bed to find the 'phone that he had left on Gorbind's bed-side cabinet. "Half five," he replied, making no attempt to stifle further yawning.

Gorbind smirked as he squinted. When he yawned, Arjun looked like a slightly devilish gargoyle. The sort you might see hanging off the eves of Notre Dame.

He had no idea where the image game from, but it did make a laugh a little.

"We've had three hours sleep," Arjun was blinking rapidly again as he looked at Gorbind.

"Dude, you're screwed," he laughed deeply as he thumped the 'phone back onto the bed-side cabinet. "You have to make it through the next twenty-four hours on only three hours sleep." He let out a deep breath as he gathered up his duvet around him to form a cocoon.

"You sure that you don't want to leg it, that Padmi is worth it?" asked Arjun; he had a rather mischievous glint in his eye.

"No, I'm not going to leg it!" he exclaimed, reaching for a pillow to launch it towards his brother. "And yes, she *is* worth it," Gorbind declared. "This twenty-four hours might be a bit rough, might be bit of a Bollywood drama. After today, I have a whole life time of Padmi. She is worth it, and don't you forget it."

Arjun parried away the pillow to raise his hands mock surrender. "Okay, fine, I believe you," he said toe-poking the pillow off his bed. "Anyone who puts up with your snoring for a whole life-time, really is worth it. "

The sound of Ardas in the kitchen suddenly became

louder and clearer as the kitchen door opened.

"GORBIND ARJUN!" yelled Nani over the sound of ardas; over the years, she had dropped the conjunction between their names. If it wasn't for their different personalities, they might have been the one person. "Get up, the both of you," her words in Punjabi rang against the walls to buffet against the bedroom door. "I am too old to drag you both down here."

Looking at Arjun, Gorbind felt his stomach flip.

Nani had looked after them both when their mother had died. His father was a gambler, a drunk and absent. As far as Gorbind was concerned, his father was a wastrel who served no purpose in the universe. He was therefore better off out of the family picture. So much so, Arvind wasn't expected to attend today. If he did, there were people instructed to make sure he was to exit stage left whilst pursed by a cousin imitating a bear.

"I said get up the pair of you," Nani repeated her imperative; there was a burr to her tone. It suggested that they ignored her words at their peril. The door slammed as she finished. The thud jolted Gorbind and hammered home her demand.

For a whole five seconds, Gorbind felt as though he was sixteen years old again; first came the bellowing, next came the dragging from his pit. He was now a grown up, and Nani too old to haul him down the stairs. It was only when he saw Arjun throw his duvet back to stand up on his badly made bed that Gorbind's train of thought derailed.

"You heard her," Arjun adopted his best superhero pose with his hands on his hips. It was a shame that he hadn't attached his bed sheet to his shirt collar and fashioned a make-shift cape.

"We need to get up, the pair of us," his brows arched dramatically. "You're getting married today. Get up; get with it, get the show on the road, sunshine."

"Come on," Arjun bent forward to pull away his duvet. "You should get showered first. You seriously honk half way to hell; you look it too." He was persistent, putting a hand to Gorbind's blue sock clad foot, Arjun tugged hard to pull him from his bed.

Unable to pose any resistance, Gorbind's limbs flailed as he was hauled off the bed. He landed with all the grace of a drunken sailor onto Arjun's makeshift bed. It was then that Gorbind caught the smell that cling to every inch of his being. The scent of stale dough, olive oil and turmeric was hard to miss. Scratching at his stubble, he looked into his palm to see dried flakes of dough. Gorbind curled his lips into a grimace; Arjun was right. He clambered across the mattress on all fours to look at his brother.

Arjun-who for reasons only be known to himself- had found his 'phone and was laughing manically. Gorbind saw the flash go off.

"Just in case," stated Arjun, beaming at him. "Evidence," he added, "That can and will be used against you, should my darling sister-in-law ever ask."

"Muppet," growled Gorbind as he got to his feet and off the blow-up mattress. "Do me a favour. Get all this tidied away," he said rubbing his palms across his face. Flakes fell to the floor as he made for the door. "Find the shewani's from the wardrobe, and we'll both get the show on the road," he glared at Arjun who was more preoccupied with sending the photo to Padmi. "Bring me some tea too."

"Yeah, yeah," nodded Arjun, not paying too much attention as he followed Gorbind out. "Two sugars, a dash of whiskey for the twice-condemned man. I'll have to make it a double, I think."

CHAPTER 40

Locking himself in the bathroom, Gorbind pulled down the toilet seat. Sitting with his head in his hands, he took a deep breath to steel himself. He was exhausted. In his gut was a hollowness from being hungry, from being more than little hungover and it throbbed with anxiety. He was actually nervous; his bones seemed to be heavier because of it. Gorbind sat up a little straighter as he passed a palm over his stomach as it growled. He had felt like this before and when he had been married the first time.

He had done the same that day too. Sat here, look at his reflection in the mirror ahead and pondered his fate.

Growling hard, his stomach really didn't take kindly to having been attacked with liberal amounts of hard spirits. Neither did the rest of him. His head throbbed and felt as though it was trapped in a vice that was slowly being tightened.

He had done this already, and with the same woman. *'How hard could this possibly be?'* he thought to himself. *'She agreed to marry you. Not just the once either, but twice. Twice, and with all the Bollywood drama that you can possibly think of. Get your act together. Get up, get into that shower.'*

Stripping off and stepping into the bath, Gorbind turned on the shower as he stood over the plug hole. As naked as the day he was born, he smelt the heady scent of the dough that he had been attacked with yesterday morning. Gorbind had been covered with the stuff; it had managed to travel, slip, into every nook and cranny. There were oil, dough and turmeric in places that should remain sacrosanct. Gorbind set about smelling and also feeling a bit more human. B reaching for Milk and Honey shower gel

Gorbind took his time; he wasn't worried too much about using all of the shower gel. This was a case of needs must. It hadn't been too bad at first. He and Nani had been in tears as she rubbed his arms with the dough mixture that was supposed to make him glow on his wedding day. When his mum's sister-his Aunty Leela-had done the same, they had both bawled their eyes out uncontrollably. Thankfully, Arjun had set things right. He had picked up a fistful of dough, added more oil, rice too and headed straight towards him like a heat-seeking missile. The small sea of Aunties that gathered around him had parted as though Moses had split the tides. What followed was a melee. Gorbind was wrestled to the ground with Arjun rubbing the dough into any and every patch of bare skin that he could find.

Afterwards, he had been well and truly plastered with the stuff. There was dough in his beard, between his toes. This was a traditional ceremony that both the bride and groom experienced. Some part of him wondered if Padmi had experienced anything similar, and whether hers had ended up with some form of pseudo-brawl with her brother. After the dough brawl, they were both barred from showering until the morning of the wedding. Nani had been really quite unequivocal about that. What she didn't know, was that Arjun had a stash of wet-wipes stowed away so that he didn't scare the kids or call in the carrion birds. One of the gathered aunties had playfully slapped his cheek and told him that he looked terrible; that with any luck the yellow, oily dough would make him look a bit more handsome come the morning.

Gorbind lathered up twice before deciding to shampoo. He also had to take care of his beard. Pulling a face in disdain, he made sure that his hair was suitably foamy. His hair he didn't mind, it was still there for the time being. The beard on the other hand, he held in contempt. It had taken such a long time to grow it, even before the civil wedding. He had suffered designer stubble for that day. All being well, it would be all gone just after lunch time. In its spikey, fuzzy, curly in places, glory, the beard was just as ceremonial as the rest of the nuptials. A few more hours and this would all be over.

Beneath his feet, the plug hole gurgled to only just mask the continued sound of his grumbling gut. Eating was probably a good idea, but he felt like hell. Lethargic really didn't cover it. Showering had freshened him up, but he still wasn't feeling sprightly. Gorbind knew he had to try, try to achieve some form of zen-like mastery as he enjoyed the heat of the water. He let the warmth seduce him, flatten out the tension between his shoulder blades and calm his nerves. Last night had been one hell of a party.

A marquee had been erected in Nani's garden so that she could host a pre-wedding get together. There had been food, dancing and enough alcohol to sink a small ship. He and Arjun had been sworn off booze. Nani had waggled her finger at both of them. That directive had most certainly been ignored. He and his brother would both have to feign not being hung over and on the pain of death. Gorbind blamed his brother entirely. Arjun had kept on handing up plastics cups.one after the other. Each one was fizzy soda laced with rum and any other spirit that he might have got his hands on. As he exhaled, he felt a horrible throb behind his ears. His little brother had a wonderful way of making things interesting and hanging the consequences. Interesting, was Arjun's middle name and Gorbind wouldn't have had him any other way.

Rinsing his hair, Gorbind ran his fingers through his dark locks to sweep them backwards against his scalp whilst removing tangles. For now, his hair was still one shade below raven with a hint of bitter chocolate. There was the odd strand of silver, but there was far more in his beard. There were splodges that twinkled at his jawline; splodges that further made having facial furniture that bit more uncomfortable. Splodges that made him feel older than he actually was.

Gorbind closed his eyes as water gushed from the shower head, cascaded down his shoulders and beyond. He closed his eyes to listen to his heart race, listen to his breath coming in and going out. He could feel the warmth of water rushing around his ankles before gurgling down the plug-hole.

All he had to do, was relax. All he had to do was get dressed, go through a few more ceremonies and get to the Gurdwara on time.

His one job, his most important job, was to turn up.

He had to turn up, take Padmi by the hand and walk

around The Guru Granth Sahib four times.

That was how he had described things to her.

He had, of course, oversimplified the whole process. Making things complicated would only make them more daunting.

Of all the things associated with them getting married, a traditional Sikh ceremony was the one thing that he had asked for. Padmi had agreed. He would get his full scale Bollywood wedding, if she could have a full scale white wedding with a frou-frou dress.

A smile flickered across his face as he looked at his left palm. With his thumb, Gorbind twirled the thick, gun-metal grey band that Padmi had wedged onto his finger. It wasn't supposed to move; only he hadn't eaten properly in the last week with the run up to today. The ring wasn't going anywhere, but he was. Ten minutes passed before he vaulted out of the bath and actually felt human.

CHAPTER 41

Hurriedly, Gorbind brushed his teeth and heard Arjun thumping his fist on the door.

"Get a move on will you!" yelled Arjun. "Your tea's going cold add I need the loo. Nani made you toast. She wouldn't let me make a fry up. I'll find you a nice greasy, breakfast burger on the way to the wedding."

Bundling on a fluffy, terry-towel robe, Gorbind barged passed his brother. He noticed a large mug of tea sat upon the stairs ready for him and picked it up.

"Could have cracked a window," grumbled Arjun closing the door and heading into the steam.

In his bedroom, Gorbind let loose the robe and pulled on a pair of dark jeans with a T-shirt. He wouldn't hear the end of it, if he traipsed down the stairs in a state of undress. Slugging the tea, Gorbind finally made his way quickly downstairs. His thundering footsteps must have alerted his grandmother, who threw open the door for him to enter the kitchen.

"Slowly, slowly," she said putting her hand to his elbow. "It's your wedding day, not Christmas. Don't you dare break your neck and today of all days; do you understand me, Gorbind?"

"Morning, Nani. Mwah!" he couldn't help but laugh as he gave her a big hug and kissed her cheek. He was unable to pull away as she cradled his face in her hands. He noticed that her eyes had filled with tears; it made his heart thud a little harder. "Same thing today, Nani," he said softly, trying to gulp down a sob that had got stuck in his throat. "Christmas came early. Not many people have two wedding days with the same person. I'm a lucky boy, I couldn't have done this without you."

Gorbind heard his grandmother tut. Bowing his head, Gorbind was almost ducking as she pulled him closer to kiss his forehead.

"Not a boy anymore," she said whispered gently. "You bring me home my granddaughter-in-law. Make your own family. I've helped you long enough. Come on, drink that tea," Nani took his hand and led him into the kitchen.

"Arjun left you cold toast, he didn't even butter it," she frowned at him, whilst shaking her head. "Eat it, then you need to get dressed. Quickly, please, Gorbind," Nani pulled out a chair for him and then bustled off towards the stove. On the hob, was a saucepan of Indian tea being kept warm on a very low flame.

He sat himself down, sipped his tea and nibbled at the cold toast. Gorbind had grown up at this table. There had been countless breakfasts eaten with sweet, spiced chai that was autumn in a cup. To this day, Nani ground her own spices for Indian tea, She would even decant some into a Tupperware box to ensure that he too could make 'proper' tea. He would drive Nani to the Indian supermarket on the other side of town just to get them.

As he polished off half a slice of toast, he gulped it down hard. He didn't have his mum today. He had no idea what might have happened if she had been here today. In raising him and Arjun, Nani had loved them, protected them. Neither he nor Arjun had gone for wanting. Nani had provided the best kind of mother's love. Nani had been heart-broken having lost her daughter; Gorbind remembered how she had given them both the biggest bear hug on the day that their mother had been killed. Nani had promised that she would do the job that his mother, Amandeep, had been prevented from doing.

In that hug, Gorbind had felt his grandmother's heart break straight down the middle. One half was for him, the other half for Arjun. He and Arjun had been trying mend it and put it back together ever since. His father was of no use; he could feel the bile rise in his throat with the mere thought of the man. A man; he was no man. His father had spent his whole life drunk as a skunk whilst bobbing in and out of betting shops.

Gorbind continued to watch his grandmother. She had plucked a robust looking blue and white mug from the cupboard and filled it with tea from the pan. At her wrist, gold bangles jangled and clinked against blue-grey stainless steel. Nani was proper old school, a colourless tumbler was dunked into the pan, and tea decanted into mug through a well-used strainer.

Gorbind couldn't have been more than six, Arjun more than two when at six in the morning they had been dragged here to Nani's. His mother had bundled up her few possessions and walked out on her husband. The night before, his father had bested half a bottle of Johnnie Walker and then turned his attention to his wife. Amandeep had collapsed upon her mother's doorstep; enough had been enough.

He remembered Arjun wailing as Nani picked her daughter up. Nani had sworn blind that with the help of the ten gurus, she would break her son-in-law's neck and send him to hell in a box if he came anywhere near them again. He had believed her; Gorbind had seen his grandmother's silver kirpan. He knew full just how fiercely protective she was. She like the thousands of Sikh Matriarchs before her, was not about to take any crap from a man blinded by his own vices. Nani had taken his mother into her arms, held her close and told her it was all over. That no one would touch her; no one would hurt a single hair on her head ever again.

Moving onto a second piece of toast, he watched Nani bustle around her kitchen. He had seen the anger in his grandmother's face. There was hurt too, that her daughter have been abused and she hadn't realised. Up to that point, the bruises and wounds inflicted by his father had been disguised or dismissed as clumsiness. Domestic abuse wasn't exactly front page news in the community. When it was so close to home, abuse could no longer be silently ignored.

In Gorbind's mind, it was a clear clarion bell to be a better, more decent human being. He had been unable to do anything as a child, but Nani had raised him and Arjun to be stronger, better men. She had made sure that they were nothing like the poor excuse for a human being that he refused to call his father. He wouldn't be around today as there was a restraining order in effect. There was no way that his father could ruin today. No flipping, way.

Gorbind inhaled more tea as Nani finally joined him. Dressed in a pale blue shalwar khameez, she was wearing a matching cardigan. She always wore a cardigan, even in the summer. Nani had heavier ones for winter; this was Nani's uniform in all weathers.

"Phatta Phut," she said wagging a finger at the plate littered with crumbs. "Finish your tea. I need to get ready too and I don't want to spend any more time running after you both. Tell Arjun to get ready to. He's not going to do this anytime soon," she pursed her lips together as she shook her head. "Gurdwara not ready yet for two boys to do this." she clapped her hand together and looked skyward. "Let's hope the Guru's help make people happy."

Rising from his seat, Gorbind nodded. "Yes, Nani. Things could change, I hope they do," he said whilst draining his mug in the sink.

He had been there when Arjun had told their grandmother that he was gay. The decision to tell her had been drawn out for months. It was only when Nani had noticed that Arjun wasn't eating, sleeping or even functioning as he wrestled with telling her. His grandmother had dragged Arjun to the kitchen table; it had been laden with all of his favourite food. He was to eat, to tell her whatever it was that was eating him up or she would smack him three ways to Sunday. Arjun had broken down at the sight of crispy, bright orange Jalebis and told Nani everything.

"May be," said Nani, blowing skin across her tea. "I hope so too. Everybody is equal in God's eyes. I love Arjun, I love God too. Arjun will always be my baby; I will always be his Nani. I don't mind that he likes boys; whatever makes him happy. Arjun's not hurting anyone."

Gorbind had heard this speech before; her words were as strong now as they had been on that day Arjun had come out. Not one thing had changed and he knew that it wouldn't. Nani loved them both completely. Her love was unconditional, it always would be.

CHAPTER 42

Leaving Nani in the kitchen, Gorbind scarpered upstairs to his room. Arjun had tidied up and laid out his wedding garb on the bed.

"Oh, God," Gorbind gulped as he took in the sight of his heavily embroidered tunic. Arjun appeared at his shoulder. He was half dressed in a white, short sleeved vest and a pair of raw silk, aubergine-coloured trousers that were tied at his waist by a golden, nylon cord. At his ankles, the fabric gathered neatly before giving way to feet that looked as though they belonged to a troll.

"Get ready quick," demanded Arjun, his hands pressed against Gorbind's shoulders. "We have half an hour before Ava and Roshni arrive with eyeliner and you get blinded by your sparkly turban."

"Fricking eyeliner," huffed Gorbind, peeling off his t-shirt and jeans. Unlike Arjun's, his own trousers were vermillion but had the same pattern on the ankles. The colour was exactly the same as what his bride would be wearing; who'd thought that there could be so many different shades of red. Red, was never just red and by any length of chalk. As he hopped around, Gorbind turned the air blue with how everything was heavy, itchy, scratchy; how he was never going to wear any of this ever again. Eventually he was handed his gold and ivory tunic that was embroidered with Paisley patterns embellished with crystals. Like Arjun, he had a vest to wear beneath it. Today would not be the day to suffer chaffing. He struggled to pull on the tunic as it was stiff and heavy. Arjun came to his aid whilst tutting and rolling his eyes. Else Gorbind had been inclined to screw the thing up into a ball and lob it out of the window.

"Slowly," Arjun batted at his hands, "Stop flipping fighting," he chided, sliding the tunic over Gorbind's head. "You asked for all of this, brother dearest," Arjun turned him around to smooth down his collar and lapels. "This is nothing. Padmi's get up is heavier, shinier and prettier than yours. At least you and I don't need our hair done or a make-up artist for that matter. Right, I need a smoke. You're on your own for a bit, I'll see you downstairs." Arjun picked up his own tunic.

"Smoke?!" shrilled Gorbind as Arjun left, leaving him feeling lost and every inch a lemon. "Don't get it anywhere near your clothes," he yelled, trying not to unleash expletives so early in the morning. Shouting and screaming would rouse Nani's attention; she'd only harangue them both. Gorbind sank heavily to his bed.

Neatly folded up, two pieces of fabric were sat upon his pillow. The one was the fabric for the turban that he was wearing today. The other was a scarf that matched the colour of his trousers. Only this second piece was far more than a scarf. Later on today, the one end of the scarf would be joined with Padmi's-she had one very similar-to form a nuptial knot. A nuptial knot that would bind them in Holy Matrimony; well and truly sealing the legal vows that they had already made.

He could feel his heart thump quicker once more over the sound of his growling guts. His stomach was rumbling with increased ferocity. Gorbind was doing the whole get dressed part. What he still had to do was get to the Gurdwara on time.

CHAPTER 43

Twenty minutes later, Gorbind traipsed downstairs clutching the turban material and the scarf. Tucked under his arm was a pair of ivory coloured shoes that curled up at the end; shoes that looked an awful lot like winkle-pickers and therein not the least bit comfortable. Gorbind moved slowly; there was something unnerving about the rustle of raw silk trousers. Arjun met him at the bottom. Gorbind caught the feint smell of burnt tobacco, but resisted making a comment.

"Chin up," whispered Arjun, taking the bundle of fabric from him. "You look like a sparkly strawberry and I'm auditioning for the human aubergine. Living room," he nudged him gently down the hall way. "Ava and Roshni are here; they've brought eyeliner."

"Lovely," he muttered as Arjun followed him. Two chairs had been positioned in the middle of the room. All around him, especially convened for the celebration was a college of Bollywood Aunties. There was glitter and sparkles everywhere as he cast his gaze around. Gorbind blinked as a camera flashed and his eyes were snatched away in quick succession. This wasn't an Indian wedding without a photographer on hand to document proceedings for all of eternity. Standing behind the two chairs were his sisters-in-law. Ava, was married to his first cousin Rohan. Roshni was married to Rohan's brother, Ajit. Their mother-in-law was his Aunty Leela, and she hovered close by with big stick of black eyeliner grasped firmly in her hand.

Feeling a nudge at this elbow, Gorbind made his way towards the chairs to sit. Arjun took the seat next to him.

"Do not swear," Arjun spoke through gritted teeth. "You are on camera. Smile, look pretty; stop scowling, smouldering or whatever you call that face. It looks a lot like a smacked bottom."

"Gorbind!" Nani bustled her way through the college of aunts. As she moved, a red scabbard and a feather plume were raised aloft; there plume was to be pinned to his turban. She had changed too and was dressed head to toe in pink. Something of a solemn silence descended in the room as Nani arrived before them. Arjun rose from his seat to exchange the turban fabric for the scabbard and plume. There was something all too practiced as he did so, not to mention a gentle reverence in the way that Arjun held the scabbard.

Gorbind was struck by the colour of Nani's outfit. Pink was very traditional; a colour worn at weddings by mothers of both the bride and the groom. Draped across Nani's head and shoulders was a pink scarf trimmed with gold brocade that had been used throughout all of the different ceremonies so far. She planted one corner of the turban fabric at his shoulder and proceeded to wrap the rest around his still damp hair to form a turban. There were more flashes from the camera, each one catching the brocade on Nani's scarf. On his head, the turban started to form; hugging his scalp close it felt tight, heavy too. Gorbind sat as still as humanly as possible, only to wince as his ears got caught. Sliding a finger between fabric and the top of his ear, he slackened off the fabric a little.

Below her breath, Nani was singing. He could hear her hum, but only just. A traditional song, something about a groom long ago. The groom had he left home to claim his bride and how all his family had celebrated on his return. There was something soothing about the song that made him forget just how tightly the turban was being wound. Nani's final flourish was to take the plume from Arjun and pin it to the high peek at the front.

Then came the eyeliner; Aunty Leela handed it over.

Ava and Roshni fulfilled their ascribed roles. They lined his eyes with black Kajal; it was supposed to ward off any evil eye that might deign to look upon him on his wedding day.

"Going to make your eyes pop," Roshni giggled wickedly whilst trying not to poke Gorbind's eyes out.

His other sister-in-law chortled and took his right eye. "I did ask Nani," she whispered through a fixed smile. "About bringing you some lovely eyeshadow, only she was having none of it. Don't worry," she added, patting his shoulder. "There's some mascara in my bag," Ava arched her brow in menace. "Waterproof and everything, should we feel teary today."

Ava pressed her finger against the tip and dabbed a splodge of black behind Arjun's ear to make him jump a little. Gorbind smiled at the unexpected attack.

A few more photographs were taken. This whole thing was more stage managed than an Oscar winning theatrical production.

All he had to do now was get to the Gurdwara.

CHAPTER 44

Travelling to the Gurdwara would only take half an hour. Gorbind had assured Padmi that he would be there. He would be on time, that everything would go by the minute by minute plan that she had emailed him and even stuck to two 'fridges. In that half an hour, his brother helped him stay relatively true to his word.

"Two breakfast rolls please," Arjun told the speaker in the wall of the drive through. "Four hash browns as well, with brown sauce."

"Red," hissed Gorbind, "We can disguise if we spill it. Brown, brown looks a bit odd."

"Red, please!" yelled Arjun as the wedding car decorated with white ribbon travelled towards the serving hatch six metres away.

Arriving at the Gurdwara, Gorbind wiped crumbs away with wet wipes. He had thoroughly enjoyed his second breakfast; the dry toast from earlier had well and truly worn off. He would however, be having a third a breakfast once he got indoors. Both he and Arjun clambered out of the car to join the rest of the Groom's party inside the langhar hall. There he was handed more food as well as more spiced tea. He had never seen so many thick pastry samosas in one place. These all came with hot spinach and onion bhajis smothered in beautifully sweet and sour tamarind chutney.

This wasn't the breakfast of a condemned man. This was the breakfast of a champion. All being well this would keep him going for a bit; it would quieten down his stomach a great deal. He wanted to get this done without his gut voicing it's disapproval at the most Holiest of moments. That really would upset the college of Bollywood aunties.

All of the anxiety that had been bubbling away in the pit of his stomach had been soaked away; such was the benefit of stodgy, deep fried, very bad for you, carbohydrates.

He was full, but could feel a hum hang in the air. It was a hum of happiness, a hum that Gorbind knew came from contentment.

Gone were the collywobbles.

Slurping the second of cup of tea that Arjun handed to him, Gorbind let out a relaxed breath to catch his eye.

Arjun smiled before giving him the all-important nod.

"Come on then," he said grabbing Gorbind's elbow. "Down the aisle you go, once again.

CHAPTER 45

Standing on the threshold of the hall, he could see the Guru Granth Sahib up ahead. Gorbind was flanked by his brother and his grandmother. Behind him were Ava, Roshni, Rohan and their younger sister Priya. Slowly, Gorbind started to travel down the walk way that divided the room in half. He focused on the Holy Book ahead as it rested upon brightly coloured cushions below a canopy.

Guru Manyour Granth

The book is the Guru.

Everything that he believed in, everything that he stood for was in the leaves of The Guru Granth Sahib. Everything that gave him courage; all that shaped the way that Gorbind saw the words filled the pages up ahead.

To the left of the canopy was a raised platform. Sat upon it were three turbaned Sikhs. In front of them were microphones, a set of tabla drums and a harmonium. The party of three were already singing with their words accompanied by the soul-stirring sound of the instruments.

Gorbind felt hands at his elbow, Arjun's foot tapped against his shin to spur him into action. He had no idea what really pushed him forward; it certainly wasn't human hands and feet. As he put one foot in front of the other, he felt as though he was gliding to arrive before the Granth. Bending to kneel, his forehead kissed the floor before he clasped his hands in prayer to rise back to his full height.

Gorbind prayed that he might be a good husband, that he and Padmi would be happy together. He asked for the faith to never hurt her, make her cry; for both of them to be strong enough to brave whatever the world might sling at them.

As he opened his eyes to refocus, the woman sat behind the Granth gave him a knowing nod.

It was time.

Taking a step back, Gorbind's feet nudged at a two metre long cushion that had been placed upon the floor. Arjun had also appeared; he took Gorbind's scabbard and handed him a garland of red and white carnations. He caught the scent of pollen drifting towards his nostrils but resisted the urge to wrinkle his nose. There was a photographer lurking. His wife wouldn't forgive him, if the album was blotted with him expelling bogey. Taking a deep breath, he turned slightly to face the door but not turn his back to the Granth.

The she was.

Padmi stood at the door, just as he had. She was flanked by her Dad, Subash, on the one side and her bother Chand on the other. Gorbind caught her mouth the word 'okay', he nodded in silent reply.

The players on the platform changed rhythm as Padmi walked down the aisle for the second time.

All he could see was Padmi, and she was floating. She was gliding down the walkway towards him. Dressed in a bright vermillion lengha, the woman he loved looked like a Goddess. As she came closer, he could the delicate sound of her anklets cut across the hymn being played on the far side. In her hands, was another flower garland.

Time felt as though it had slowed down to a complete stop as she arrived by the cushion. Padmi handed her brother her garland, before kneeling and bowing to the Granth as he had done. Chand handed back the flower garland as she rose.

Gorbind and Padmi were then toe to toe once more.

This was the second time in as many weeks.

As Padmi lifted her hands to drape the garland around his neck, Gorbind took a slight step back.

There as brief moment of quiet laughter for a gag that played out at most weddings.

Stepping forward, Gorbind bowed his head. His six foot one inch frame was within range, and Padmi was able to garland him with ease. It was his turn next, and no gag this time. Briefly, Gorbind held her hands. She wove her fingers between his, to give a gentle, reassuring squeeze.

"Breathe," she whispered, her eyelashes fluttered below a red and white bejewelled brow. "Nearly there, lovely. Focus, Gorbind, focus."

Less than two months ago, he had reminisced with Padmi about how this had all started. Five years on, he could barely believe how much they had experienced with one another.

Keeping her hand in his, Gorbind turned to face the canopy. Her fingers were warm and she kept a tight hold of his hand. He didn't want to let go; not now, not ever. Gorbind bit his lip as Padmi fiddled with his wedding band. He wasn't sure if this was supposed to ground him or distract him.

There were a few words of welcome, they both sat to listen. A distinct air of contemplation filled the air before he was asked to stand for Ardas. This was the prayer that signalled the start of the ceremony.

The giani-he who was presiding over the ceremony-went through a number of proclamations and declarations. Gorbind stood as his grandmother, his in-laws stood to acknowledge that they were here to witness their child and grandchild undertake the sacrament of marriage. The congregation were told how Padmi was brought here today carried on love as she left her home and family to join Gorbind. From the corner of his eye, he could see Nani clutching a folded up piece of kitchen roll. Nani was both his mother and father today. She had fulfilled the promises that had made to his mother. Her job was now done.

Then the time came for the proverbial knot to be tied; the nuptial knot.

Subash stepped forward to sit between them. Draped across Gorbind's shoulder's was a red scarf, Padmi wore one two. Taking one of each, Subash tied them both together using three knots.

He was her. She was his. They were together.

From now on, they were one. A perfect whole.

Gorbind had watched his father-in-law carefully. For the second time, he was giving his daughter away. Once the knot was tied, the two of them shook hands. Neither one of them said anything. Subash had given away his greatest treasure.

Together he and Padmi would step towards their future as a married couple. Gorbind held her hand as they circled the Guru Granth Sahib four times. They walked once to let go of their separate pasts. A second time for their marriage to have joy. Third, to have a love that binds them together and fourth for their faith in each other and God.

Everything that happened next was something of a sparkly blur. There was a reception later, but first he had to formally escort Padmi away from her parental home. As he walked her out, Gorbind felt the worst husband in the world. Padmi struggled to bite back tears and sobs as she threw rice behind her into each of the four corners. The idea being that whilst she was leaving, the home would still be happy, healthy and prosperous.

When Chand closed the car door, Padmi had broken down entirely; she had become a vermillion-coloured puddle in his arms as they sped off. Holding her close, Gorbind could feel her sob and shudder as one chapter of life closed to start another. He said nothing as they arrived at the reception venue. There, they were supposed to shower, change; Gorbind planned to shave and get rid of his horrible beard. He would however spend forty-five minutes lying on the bed of the honey-moon suite with Padmi crying into his shoulder.

Once he had wiped away her tears, they found themselves laughing and in stitches as they both clambered out of their traditional wedding outfits. Gorbind sat in an armchair in his blue socks and matching boxers. Padmi sat on the edge of their bed in rather pricey looking purple underwear. Rather incongruously, her red and white bridal bangles remained on her wrists.On the other side of the room, hanging from the wardrobe was his blue tuxedo and Padmi's matching ball gown that shone with crystals dotted on yards of floaty tulle.

"Don't be drinking all the bubbles," said Gorbind, his eyes squinting as he looked at Padmi side long.

"Stay away from the rum," chided Padmi. "You'd end up with a two day hangover, and in two days we fly. You're a soppy drunk, but incredibly moody when hungover." She half smiled, as slowly her gaze moved from his face and travelled to his socks.

Arching his brows, Gorbind pursed his lips together. It took him a moment to work out what she was thinking. He had never moved so fast as he ran towards his wife.

They would be late to the reception. Such was the benefit of a wedding synchronised to Punjabi time; a delay was built into the plans. No one was going to bat an eyelid.

CHAPTER 46

"Remind me again," Padmi glanced over her shoulder to half yell at him. "Which key is it? Oh, balls," she cursed further as the keys clattered onto the floor with a thud.

Gorbind heard the swearing and thud as he closed the boot. He had also seen Padmi juggle with two aloe vera plants, and a slender two-pint bottle of milk. A pizza carton sat on the floor near the welcome mat.

"Wait!" he screamed back. He shook his head as he wheeled two suitcases to the kerb. "Don't you go any further, Missis. Not so much as a single step, okay?"

"What, why?" queried Padmi, about to scoop up the keys. For two seconds, she genuinely looked scared.

"I'll tell you," Gorbind trundled the suitcases to position them right next to Padmi's very scuffed trainers. He bent to pick up the keys, tapping her hands out the way. Once up right, he put the key in the door to unlock it. Still he said nothing, as he pushed the door open with a flat palm.

He was conscious that Padmi was eyeing him with both suspicion and curiosity. "Brace," he said smirking. Gorbind rubbed his palms together in menace.

"Eh?" Padmi couldn't get much more out as Gorbind nudged the back of her knees. Knocking her off balance, he was able to scoop her up into his arms.

He moved quickly. Partly to prevent protest, but mostly so that he could get Padmi over the threshold without suffering a black eye and a possible hernia. Gorbind winced as Padmi had held both his skin and shirt beneath her fingers. Biting his lip, he stamped his feet down hard once he had crossed his threshold. He half let go of Padmi's legs, but guided down the rest of her as she clung on for dear life.

"What the flip was that?" she asked, uncurling her limbs to get to her feet. Padmi quickly disengaged her arms and legs.

Gorbind had actually felt her heart race; he'd also felt her rather sweaty palms.

"Tradition," he replied, rubbing a palm across where Padmi had dug her nails in. "I've only ever done that when you've bordered on being hammered. Now you're sober and also my wife. A double whammy basically."

"Sshh," Padmi grabbed his shirt once again. She looked through the door, both ways. "Don't tell the whole world that I was hammered."

Gorbind chucked quietly as he prized away her fingers. She had this unnerving ability to always grab a fistful of flesh. "But you almost were," he said pulling her into his arms. He splayed his digits across the curve of her backside and against scratchy denim. If she ever asked him how big it was, he knew that lying was going to be useful. "You were almost completely, utterly trolleyed, my dearest wife."

"Bring in my bags," she said, pulling away and looked quite abashed.

"Yes, dear," sighed Gorbind as she sulked down the hall. He looked at the all the stuff left on the door step.

This was it.

They were about to try for domestic bliss.

What could possibly go wrong?

CHAPTER 47

"GOR-BIND!"

His eyes snapped open at hearing his name being yelled. Gorbind felt his stomach flip. Jabbing his elbows into the sofa, he got to his feet. Given how chaotic the last few days had been, falling asleep wasn't exactly a cardinal sin. The last that he remembered, he had been here with Padmi and they had both landed on the sofa in a heap.

So where was she, he was here alone?

No doubt the sound of cupboards being opened and closed in the kitchen had something to do with it.

He would have to investigate; pushing the kitchen

door open, he saw Padmi making something of a mess.

On the worktop were a handful of peppers that were starting to wrinkle. A courgette sat next to them; it looked equally ropey. He further noted a jar of pasta sauce. Saying nothing, he took a mental inventory. There were brown skinned onions, a clove of garlic that had started to sprout. With the wedding kicking off, grocery shopping had fallen right down his list of priorities. He had effectively decamped to Nani's. What he hadn't thought about was this. With flights booked for honeymoon in the morning, he had hoped that leftover pizza would cover things. He didn't want to make a mess of the house, if he didn't have to.

"Do you have a colander?" asked Padmi, pouring Farfalle into a pan of boiling water.

Having noted all of the ingredients, he slowly scanned the rest of his kitchen. All around, doors were ajar, tea-towels had be cast aside. She had also managed to half fill his sink with dishes. He eventually centred on Padmi standing squarely in the middle of it.

Had he slept for half an hour or two days?

"Well, do you?" she asked, stepping forward she picked up a pasta spoon from a holder. She held it very much like a spanner.

"Whatcha doin?" he asked, moving his eyes from the pasta spoon with its red handle. It was same shade as Padmi's bangles. Eventually, he made eye contact.

"Cooking," she replied, her lashes fanning. For some daft reason, she had applied semi-permanent extensions for the wedding. "But I asked first. Do you have a colander?"

Tentatively, Gorbind stepped across the kitchen and liberated the pasta spoon. He had to tug it firmly from her grip. "I do, yes," he replied, stirring the pasta.

"Do you want to tell me where it is?" His wife slid off, opening more cupboards.

Gorbind held up his palm. His wedding band flashed; the still very new ring, caught some of the sun that streamed in through a bay window. He put down the spoon, and counted to six in his head. "Padmi, this is my kitchen," he said carefully.

Padmi glowered back at him, crossing her arms. "You mean *our* kitchen, Gorbind," her tone was level, but did have a slight burr to it.

"It is now, yes," Gorbind felt a bitter pang as he conceded. "Crap, how do I say this?" he groaned as he briefly squeezed his eyes shut.

His wife was not looking best pleased. "Politely,

perhaps?" she offered. "Bit early for divorce, Mr.Phalla. But go on." She edged closer, her eyes narrowed. "I know you're domesticated. You've always cooked when I've stayed. Guess this is negotiation," Padmi hooked a finger into the belt hook of his jeans.

"I am domesticated,yes," Gorbind half shrugged. "Stupidly territorial too. I've never had to share a kitchen, well this place, with anyone. I know how to use it, how to pass a vacuum around the joint. My bathroom, it's spotless. I am now going to live with a woman, who can do all the above too. I feel as though I am giving up half my kingdom."

"Stop right there," Padmi pressed a finger to his lips. "You're not giving up half your kingdom, sweetheart. You're sharing it. You're sharing the whole damned thing. Okay, so you make a pretty good veggie lasagne. Yet you wear old socks, your shirts are never ironed properly. Don't get me started on that garden-" her other hand flicked towards the window, causing her bridal bangles to jangle. "This is not an invasion, Gorbind. This is a joint occupation."

Joint occupation. He let the words enter his mind and sit for a few moments.

"If I cook, clean," he offered. "Keep the toilet seat down, don't roll in at three. Will you try not to burn my shirts, throw out my socks but sort my garden out?"

Padmi laughed quietly. She tilted her head slightly, as though faking consideration.

"Joint occupation," she repeated, releasing his belt hook and clamping her hands together at the base of his spine.

Joint occupation. She had a deal.

Epilogue

It was the scent that got Gorbind. Perfume that clung to the chunky knit mink coloured scarf as it was placed delicately into an evidence bag. There were other items, harvested away from the deceased. The body of whom had been placed with gentle reverence upon autopsy room table. Her dignity was preserved by a light weight pale blue sheet and he watched in silence as it was drawn up and over her face. His first thought was that of a sleeping angel, lying in repose in between missions from The Almighty. His second thought had been of his own daughter, his little girl. He could not even dare to think of a world where she did not exist. Gorbind made a mental note to hug his daughter a little closer when he clocked off later.

Even now and after a good few years on the job,

seeing dead bodies lain out so cold filled him with a sense of heavy unease. All he could do was to paint on a cold exterior that gave the impression of being barely human. This allowed him some distance to do his job as best he could. The downside was the joke amongst his colleagues that he was part android and without feeling.

He was here to get a few more details. There was a witness waiting at the station, a friend of the deceased young woman. Gorbind's heart missed as beat as she was being taken away to be placed into cold iciness of storage.

It was down to Gorbind to interview the witness and get a picture of the rather tragic events that had led him to be here.

He was about to leave and through strips of colourless plastic that hung at the door when something else caught his attention. Sat on a grey metal tray was a pair of glasses. Thick framed and fashionably so; the one lens was fractured and corresponded to the deceased eye being an oxidised red mess as the socket had caved in. Sat next to the tray was another bag, containing a duffel coat that must have been a little damp. With evaporation, vapour had misted up the bag as it cooled.

Rubbing a palm across his stubble clad tense jaw, Gorbind centred himself to leave. He still had his daughter, he held onto that fact within his head. A couple of colleagues had been despatched to the young lady's parents to deliver the news that every parents hoped that they would never hear.

When he did arrive home, the first thing he did was go the nursery.

She was nearly four. It wasn't a nursery anymore, but the name had stuck. His little girl was curled up beneath a duvet emblazoned with unicorns. Kneeling beside her bed, Gorbind moved a stray lock of chocolate brown hair that fallen across her nose. Kissing the ends of his fingers, he placed the kiss onto her cheek.

"I love you, my little baby mango," he said quietly. "I love to the moon and back." Tip-toeing out, Gorbind closed the door behind him to enter his bedroom.

He knew not to switch the light on. Through the shadows, he saw the duvet move. His wife looked at him through a mass of dark locks that matched his daughter's. Her expression was that of curiosity; as though checking to make sure he was there and not some will o' the wisp.

Gorbind stuck out his tongue and blew a raspberry.

"Muppet," grumbled his wife, retreating back below the covers.

He lowered himself slowly, silently into bed, into the warmth Padmi's arms.

Kangana

ABOUT THE AUTHOR

Punam Farmah is a teacher of Psychology and Social Sciences with horticultural tendencies, a trained listener, and lives in Birmingham, England. She is very appreciative of the help from the rest of her family and acknowledges that without them, this book would be devoid of any words, motivation or happy thoughts. When not teaching or experimenting with the plot, she rather likes Star Trek, Shakespeare, the Whedon-verse as well as seeing what can be made with the preserving pan.

Printed in Great Britain
by Amazon